Her Mother's Ashes 2

More Stories by South Asian Women
in Canada and the United States

Her Mother's Ashes 2

More Stories by South Asian Women in Canada and the United States

edited by
Nurjehan Aziz

TSAR
Toronto
1998

TSAR Publications
P. O. Box 6996, Station A
Toronto, Ontario
M5W 1X7 Canada

We acknowledge the support of the Canada Council for the Arts for our publishing program. We also acknowledge support from the Ontario Arts Council.

Acknowledgement is made to the following publications for permission to publish some of the stories in this anthology: "Wake Up" by Shani Mootoo, from *Out On Main Street*, Press Gang Publishers, Vancouver, Canada, 1993; "The Cat Who Cried" by Shauna Singh Baldwin, from *English Lessons and Other Stories*, Goose Lane Editions, Fredericton, New Brunswick, Canada, 1996.

Cover art by Rossitza Skortcheva

CANADIAN CATALOGUING IN PUBLICATION DATA

Main entry under title:

Her mother's ashes 2: more stories by South Asian women in Canada and the United States

ISBN 0-920661-63-7

1. Short stories, Canadian (English) – Women authors.*2. Short stories, Canadian (English) – South Asian-Canadian authors.* 3. Short stories, American – Women authors. 4. Short stories, American – South Asian American authors. 5. Canadian fiction (English) – 20th century.* 6. American fiction – 20th century. I. Aziz, Nurjehan.

PS8329.H47 1998 C813'.01'089287 C98-932983-6
PR9197.33.W65H47 1998

Printed and bound in Canada

Contents

Preface

There has been such a diverse and continued expression of interest in South Asian women's writing in Canada and the United States that a second anthology, especially one that includes younger women, was conceived. This collection brings together seventeen authors, and presents as much or greater diversity than the previous volume, *Her Mother's Ashes and Other Stories by South Asian Women in Canada and the United States.*

Some of the questions that arise in such a collection are: how strong is a South Asian sensibility, and how far does it adapt to countries of adoption; how far does it transgress boundaries? A discussion of these considerations can be found in Arun Prabha Mukherjee's introduction to the first volume, and is also for the reader to ponder from the stories presented here.

From another point of view, there seems to be a strong South Asian identity, or consciousness, judging by the generous consent of the writers to be included in such an anthology.

I would like to express my deep gratitude to my husband Moyez for his tremendous support for and overall involvement with this project. As before, his suggestions and comments have been most helpful. My grateful thanks also to Roshni Rustomji for spreading the word among the American writers, and to Selena Tandon for help in the production of the book.

Nurjehan Aziz
Toronto, November 1998

The Mango Tree

SHREE GHATAGE

Mina, my younger sister, had just announced her engagement and even though the official exchange of rings was two months away, the celebrations began early. Our friend Laila was the first to host a party. I deliberately arrived late, still out of sorts with Mina because her decision to marry Ravi had been so sudden, so unexpected. She had been spending Christmas and New Year's Eve at Papa's coffee estate, and on New Year's day, 5 AM, she phoned us with her news. She sounded as if she'd been partying all night.

"What do you mean?" I said into the receiver when it was my turn to speak. I'd gathered the gist of her announcement by the exclamations and gasps of delight that had emanated from Ma, Akka, and Mai who had been snatching the phone from each other in excitement. "What do you mean, you're getting married. Didn't you *always* say you would *never* go in for an arranged marriage?"

Mina laughed. "I know I did," she said, "but I got so fed up of listening to Aunt Krishna's 'Ravi is from a top-notch family, a fun-tastic person, fair and handsome' a thousand times, that I finally agreed to meet this paragon. And it's just as well I did!" She sounded breathless and coy, unlike her thirty-something self.

"But you and I, we always said arranged marriages weren't our cup of tea: too old-fashioned!" I insisted.

"The arranged part wasn't that bad, Gita, really. No one asked me to sing a song or list my accomplishments and *no one* vanished, leaving Ravi and me to privately discuss God knows what. On the contrary, our meeting was quite civilized. Papa and I, Ravi and his family sipping afternoon tea under Aunt Krishna's rain tree in her rose garden. In fact, Aunt Krishna did say she has someone in mind for you. Maybe—"

"Don't try and convert me, Mina, I want nothing arranged-far-ranged."

"I bet you didn't go out last night," Mina said, obviously intent on making her point. When I didn't answer, she continued, "See! There are just no eligibles left in Bangalore, and if you don't try to meet someone the way I did—"

"It's no good, Mina," I said, thrusting the phone into Ma's hand. Akka and Mai were chanting thanksgiving prayers in the puja room: when it came to communicating with Lord Venkatesh, my grandmother and grandaunt took second place to none.

Mina returned to Bangalore the following week, and when she introduced Ravi to us I had to admit she could not have made a better choice. He passed muster with Ma, Akka, Mai and myself the very first time we met him—a difficult feat given the fact that the only thing the women in our household agree upon is to disagree.

Now here I was at Laila's, surrounded by young couples and toddling children and fat bouquets of freshly cut flowers. I caught Laila's eye. She came forward and told me her cousin Kishore was here and would I like to meet him? I nodded. She had spoken warmly of him in the past and the glint in her eye had told me there was a conspiracy here, to forge alliances. My curiosity was piqued.

We found Kishore in the balcony, standing alone. He smiled at us and I wondered whether my meeting him was the result of a favourable configuration of stars the astrologer had recently told me about. I noticed his skin was leathery and tanned and his midriff had seen leaner years. But before I could jump to any conclusions, I cautioned myself: Don't be put off by what you see. After all, the areas around your eyes are taking on a darker hue, tiny moles are beginning to appear on your arms, and how many times have you caught yourself saying: "That would have been twenty years ago," while referring to events that took place in school.

Kishore and I filled our dinner plates and returned to the balcony. He obviously enjoys a good joke, I noted, watching him respond to the banter in the room. And when the conversation turned to mystery novels, he joined in with enthusiasm, saying his preference was for the thickly plotted ones. And when I said Agatha Christie's flimsy mysteries ought really to have been written as stories, Arthur Conan Doyle-style, he wholeheartedly agreed.

We met several times over the next few weeks, sometimes over dinner, sometimes for long evening drives that culminated in chickoo ice cream cones or pineapple juice or maghai paan. He told me his parents lived in Cochin and had been after him to settle down for some time now; he said he'd mentioned me to them. I didn't respond to this statement but told him about my job as a tour guide with Crown Travels instead, about our five-women joint-family setup, Ma, Akka, Mai, Mina and myself here in Bangalore, and Papa two hours north of us at his coffee estate in Pennamai.

It was the season for open-air concerts. I couldn't think of any other person I would prefer to sit under the stars with, as we sat listening to the sitar player spin music centuries old, as I watched Kishore's long fingers keep rhythm to the beat of the tabla.

One March night, after we had finished eating dinner at his cricket club, I asked Kishore whether he would like to visit our house, meet the eccentric women who resided there. He nodded, seemed pleasantly surprised.

"Maybe if we leave right away, they'll be downstairs," I said, suddenly impatient to make the introduction. "That is, they won't be changed for bed." Kishore quickly cancelled our coffee order, drove me home. Then, instead of opening his car door and coming around to open mine, he turned in my direction and stroked my cheek. I dropped my eyes. He mustn't have noticed my interlocked fingers clenching into a tighter basket for now his hand was trailing downwards, contouring my thigh; I could feel its weight, the penetrating warmth of his palm. My eyes swept upwards, stopped at his nose. I pulled away abruptly, ran into the house.

Damn, damn, damn, Kishore is definitely not impressed by my pathetic school-girl prudery, I berated myself, remembering his eyes, unyielding and distant in the moment I had looked at him before jumping out of the car. I brushed past Mai and Akka—their busy, unerring instinct for crisis drawing them to the front door—and ran upstairs. Why must I always notice noses, I despaired, standing on the balcony, looking down at the empty driveway; why did I notice Kishore's? Flaring nostrils look noble on a woman, feminine on a man.

My entire nose obsession was to do with Uncle Sudhir, of course, his wet, hairy nose bruising my soft cheeks. I was sure my aversion for his nose had produced this awkward tendency within me to notice all and condemn most noses. I always disliked Uncle Sudhir. Even as a little girl, every time I heard his voice at the front door asking for Ma, I would run into the garden, crawl into the shed until Mai was sent to fetch me. Then I would have to go in, suffer his embrace. Plucking the treat from his hand, I would glare at Mina, perched on Ma's lap, her legs swinging, face smeared with chocolate. Resenting her for being won over by Uncle Sudhir's measly peace offering, I would hide my bar under a bush until our gardener's son came home in the evening when I would give it to him. I wanted nothing from Uncle Sudhir.

There was no point in me waiting in the balcony: Kishore wasn't coming back. I went into my bedroom and locked the door. A short while later I heard Ma, Mai and Akka walking up the stairs, discussing Mina's engagement menu. Only three days left for the big ring exchange and still no consensus regarding the food. Mai was insisting that at least one of the five sweetmeats prepared that day had to be Papa's favourite. The way menu stands now, not one sweet, she complained, not one sweet will he be able to eat. I didn't hear the end of the argument because they entered Ma's room at the other end of the corridor. Soon Papa will be here for the engagement: the thought was suddenly comforting.

Determined not to replay in my head the latter end of the night's events, I looked at the shadow of the trembling bougainvillaea brushing the face of my wall clock and forced myself to think about Papa and the summer holidays Mina and I used to spend with him at his coffee estate, in Pennamai. We'd accompany Papa on his daily rounds of the plantation, sit with him in his office as he conducted the business of the day. We would meet the workers and their families who had lived on the estate for generations; play cricket and hares and hounds with their children. We would feed the cattle in the farmhouse; watch Appu, the farmhand, milk the cows.

I remembered clearly the plaintive lowing of fattened cattle, the acrid smell of newly dropped, steaming dung. I suddenly longed for the taste of warm, fresh, unboiled milk, white, frothy, rising up, spilling over brims of tall steel tumblers. I wished I could go back. Or maybe not, I thought, remembering that summer holidays were always tainted by the fact that Ma drove down to the estate only for the weekends and when she did there were adult gatherings all the time: lunch parties, card parties, dance parties. Until that holiday when I was ten years old, after which Ma stopped coming to the estate altogether.

That summer she phoned us often, promising to drive down soon. Akka isn't well, she explained, and needs looking after. Every Saturday morning, instead of going to the market with Papa and Mina, I would wait for Ma's car to pull up in the driveway; it never came. Then, when the holidays were coming to an end, Ma said she would come the last weekend to bring us back to Bangalore in time for school. The evening before she was expected, Ma walked into our bedroom. Mina was fast asleep in her cot. Ma knelt by my bed and held me so close that I could hear the rapid knocking of her heart. She ran her fingers through my curls and tangling them, said: "Who's been telling you all these things?"

"It hardly matters now! Did you or didn't you?" Papa had followed Ma into the room. I could scarcely recognize his tight voice.

"My aunt and my mother live with me. Did you ask them? Or is it just your sister who spies—"

"Did you or didn't you?" Papa was whispering behind clenched teeth.

Ma moved away from me, sat back on her haunches, and still not looking at Papa, said, "Don't ever ask me what I do with my time and I won't ask you what you do with yours. You will not move to the city and I will not live here where nothing ever happens. Let's leave it at that."

Ma's face looks so flushed, I thought, just like a hard puri after Cook has overfried it. Papa's face looks just like Mina's does, after an argument with Ma: angry, disappointed, hurt. After glancing at Mina who was breathing evenly, Papa left the room.

That night Ma slept with me in my bed and I held her tightly, not wanting to let her go, not understanding my fierce need to hold her there, forever. Through the years the details of that night became somewhat blurred but one memory did not lose its sharpness: the scent on Ma that night was the smell of Uncle Sudhir, the sweet-cloying perfume of his gardenia attar.

The bougainvillaea creeper outside my window had stopped rustling. Soon, the sky would change colour, the birds would take wing, the gardener would broom the yard. For now everything was still. I must have fallen asleep then, because the next time I opened my eyes the conviction which had formed the backbone of my shifting dreams was now on my tongue: "Kishore was my last chance and now that I've lost him, every hope of my getting married is dashed, khatam, demolished."

The clock showed 9 AM. I rushed into the bathroom and after getting dressed hurried out of the house, shouting out to whoever was listening that I would be back in time for lunch.

I pulled into the front porch of Carlton Hotel. Mr Jeevan, a regular client of Crown Travels, was waiting outside; he made a sign for me to park the car. I walked up to him and apologized for being late. He nodded his head in an irritated fashion and introduced me to Mr Haroun, explaining to me that it was Mr Haroun's first visit to the city. Before I could say anything, he told Mr Haroun that he had arranged with Crown Travels to give him an excellent tour. Mr Jeevan assured his guest that I was recommended to him as an "intelligent girl with very good knowledge of sights . . ." Listening to his apologetic tone, I wondered whether Mr Jeevan had asked for a male tour guide and had got me instead.

Mr Haroun was making his way towards a waiting car. Several people rushed forward to open the door for him; he appeared not to notice. The car was luxurious in its size and coolness and I slipped in beside him. Mr Jeevan took the front seat, next to the driver.

I told the driver to take us to the Botanical Garden on Trunk Road and turned to Mr Haroun. He was dressed for the desert in a long, white, flowing gown; his head was covered with a white cloth, held down by a black ring that circled his crown. Dark glasses completely obscured his eyes.

"Sir! How do you like Bangalore, popularly known as Garden City?" I smiled.

"Ahem, Huzoor?" Mr Jeevan turned his head and smiling at Mr Haroun, said, "First we go to Garden, then Vidhan Saudh Assembly

Hall, then I'm making arrangements to have lunch with diamond merchant in spacious house. Afternoon . . ." His voice tapered off.

Does Huzoor not talk, I wondered. I wasn't sure, didn't know what I was doing in this car, sitting next to this man who appeared to be deaf. And maybe blind, judging by the dark glasses wrapped around his eyes. There was pressure building up in my lower back. I looked outside the window. Kishore's pursed mouth and disappointed eyes stared back at me.

"Huzoor? First we'll go . . ." I wished Mr Jeevan would shut up.

"Garden only." Mr Haroun spoke.

"What . . .?"

"Garden only," I repeated, my voice echoing dry authority.

"Yes, yes!" Mr Jeevan smiled, concealing well his annoyance at the disruption of his plans. There goes his cut with the diamond merchant, I thought. Even now the merchant's wife and daughters must be busy in the kitchen, adding saffron to well-spiced mutton biryani, frying onions and cashewnuts for the garnish. I could almost smell the crusty, pungent aroma of mince samosas.

The car pulled up outside the Botanical Gardens. Mr Jeevan jumped out of the car to open Mr Haroun's door.

"There's an almond tree." So, I thought, Huzoor talks to women. He was pointing to a large tree that was shading the entrance booth.

"A mango tree, you mean," I said, politely.

"No, almond tree."

"No, sir. That is a mango tree." After the coolness of the car, the heat was making my head throb. Mr Jeevan was frowning at me not to press the issue. I was quite willing to let it drop.

"No, that is almond tree—Jeevan, next time hire someone who knows what almond tree looks like!"

You pompous fool, I wanted to say to him, you arrogant Mr Huzoor, you shouldn't have chosen a mango tree to quarrel about. There is a grove of mango trees in our backyard. Under one tree stands a wooden swing so old, it creaks dangerously if anyone tries to sit on it. It wasn't always so, for when I was a baby, Ma would place me in a cloth hammock tied to its four cables and when the swing moved, pushed by a breeze, the small hammock would rock gently. I would lie there all morning, sometimes dozing, sometimes awake, the shadows of the leaves caressing my face, sunshine playing hide-and-seek with my body. Don't tell me I don't know what a mango tree looks like, Mr Huzoor. I've scraped my knees climbing them. My school dictionary still holds between its pages pressed mango leaves, once shiny and emerald green, now frail, dull and spotted. The pressed flowers must be somewhere on Papa's estate, glued to the letters I wrote him week after week. Don't tell me this mango tree is an almond tree, you insufferable ignoramus.

"See the lance-shaped leaves, the large clusters of small pink flowers: that, sir, is a mango tree." I forced an impersonal tone. Moving forward, I read the label nailed into its trunk. "Genus: Mangifera. Mango tree."

"Mango tree!" I called after their disappearing backs and followed them through the entrance into the garden.

Mr Jeevan and Huzoor were sitting on a bench. They were discussing something; it was obvious my services were not required. I walked back to the car and got into the front seat. I left the door open; although it was parked in the shade, the inside felt like a warm tandoor.

I wished I could see Papa today. It was a long time since I'd visited Pennamai and longer still since he had come to Bangalore. I decided I would call him at lunchtime, persuade him to drive down tonight for dinner. I would keep his coming as a surprise for Mina and Ravi. They got along so well together: father and his prospective son-in-law. I lowered the window pane and banged shut the car door. Ravi and Mina are on everyone's minds, I thought, remembering the recent phone call I had received from our cousin Rekha in Madras. Rekha had never called long distance before. "Is everything all right?" I asked.

I don't know, she said, then proceeded to tell me that she had just heard that Ravi had gotten a girl into trouble in college days, a long time ago. It seemed Ravi had offered to marry the girl but she had refused, preferring to . . . you know, how should she put it, terminate it. She had heard this from someone who used to be with Ravi in college. Didn't know whether it was just a rumour. She was calling us because she felt she had to tell the family what she knew *before* Mina's engagement, in case anything went wrong afterwards . . . Ma would then say to her, "Why didn't you tell us, Rekha? Before the wedding!"

I told Rekha I didn't think there was a need to bring it up with Mina or anybody else because everything had happened so long ago. Rekha agreed instantly and before putting the phone down, said, "That Madhuri-something did have a reputation . . . I remember hearing her name in a similar context before."

The men were getting into the car. Mr Jeevan was grinning: their business talk must have been fruitful. When we returned to the hotel, I turned around to wish Huzoor a happy stay; he was reaching inside the pocket of his robe. Not wanting his baksheesh envelope, I quickly said goodbye.

I phoned Papa the minute I walked into the house. He's away for the day and not expected back till after dinner, his cook told me. Ma was in the sitting room, going through the guest list for Mina's engagement. I told her about Huzoor, the incident regarding the mango tree.

"Which garden did you take him to?" Ma said.

"The one on Trunk Road," I answered, sitting on the sofa opposite.

Ma lowered the list. "I've been there—" she began.

"I just called Papa. It seems he's away for the day."

"He'll be here tomorrow, Gita. Aunt Krishna is driving down with him."

I bumped my knee on the coffee table as I stood up.

"Have your lunch first, then go and take a bath, Gita. You look exhausted. Have a nap afterwards. It'll make you feel better," Ma said, peering into the list once again.

"What do you mean better? There's nothing the matter with me."

Ma didn't reply.

I went to the dining room. I must have really looked exhausted because Mai and Akka made a fuss over me and told the serving boy to replenish my plate before it was empty. When I got up from the dining table, all I wanted to do was lie down. I wasn't optimistic about the napping bit because my earlier conviction regarding Kishore and my future was now hammering on my nerves.

I awakened several hours later to find the sky had turned dark and the rising moon was casting weak shadows on my bed. After a quick bath, I went downstairs.

Ravi was there and everyone was seated at the dining table. Ma was plying food into Ravi's plate, refusing to take "no" for an answer. Akka and Mai were their usual fussing selves, but tonight there was a sparkle in their eyes: Ravi was their very first grandson-in-law. They knew by heart his food preferences, the short list of his dislikes. Akka felt a special affinity for him because he abhorred brinjal, just like she did: that vegetable tickles the roof of my mouth, she claimed. Mai was flattered because he loved chutneys and pickles—can't eat a meal without them, Ravi assured her; chutneys and pickles were her specialty. Looking at Mina's flushed face, a thought registered itself in my head: the mood I am in tonight is identical to the mood I was in that last weekend of the summer holidays, when I was ten years old.

That holiday, Ma drove down to the estate Friday night. Saturday, the house was full of visitors: women in bright, cotton saris, men in tennis whites, complaining how boring the summer had been without her. But, in spite of the nonstop chatter ringing through our house, the silence between Ma and Papa lay like a stodgy lump in my throat. Sunday morning, all of us were waiting for Mina on the front porch, ready to make the farewell round of the estate before leaving for Bangalore. Papa was impatient. Gita, go see where on earth Mina can be, he said. I found her in the dining room, cutting a silver star from a comic book. When she proved oblivious to being hurried up, I rocked the big mahogany chair in which she was kneeling so violently that it toppled over. Mina's wrist was fractured and had to be put in a cast. I waited for a severe dressing-down from Ma and Papa: it never came. Mina didn't say anything but I knew if I hadn't rocked the chair so hard, she wouldn't have fallen and hurt herself so badly. Consumed by guilt, I made a decision not to eat jaggery stick jaws for one whole year and vowed that I would never be mean, to anyone, ever again.

After an enormous meal fit for a son-in-law, Mina, Ravi and I sat in the drawing room having second helpings of sweet rice kheer. Ma, Akka and Mai had retired to bed.

I wanted to tell Mina about the previous night, about Huzoor and the mango tree. But ever since that fateful meeting with Ravi under Aunt Krishna's spreading rain tree, it was as though Mina had entered a different world and the connecting door had been banged shut in my face.

"Gita, you've been so quiet," Mina said. She and Ravi were sitting close to each other.

I didn't answer and looking at Ravi, said, "I believe you know someone by the name of Madhuri?"

"Madhuri who?" Mina asked.

"Someone I knew a long time ago," he answered slowly, his gaze fixed on the french windows leading into the back garden.

"I've never heard you mention her," Mina said.

"Haven't you? As I said, I knew her a very long time ago. In college. Before IIM."

"How is it that you know her, Gita?" It seemed Mina wanted to get to the bottom of this.

"I *don't* know her—" I said.

"So why did you ask Ravi!"

"It's just that someone I met the other day mentioned Madhuri was in Ravi's college. Same science batch, I believe—in any case, it's not important . . ." I yawned. "I'm really sleepy. I think I'll go to bed." I left the room.

"Who is this Madhuri, anyway?" I heard Mina ask.

I hesitated outside wondering whether I should go back in, concoct something for Mina. It wasn't too late: Ravi was taking his time replying.

"A long time ago . . . when I was in college . . ." I heard him say.

I continued up the stairs.

"What did you think you were doing?" Mina was standing over me. She clicked on my bedside lamp. I ran my tongue over my teeth: they tasted bitter, gritty.

"Well?" Mina twitched my counterpane, "Why couldn't you have just told *me* about Madhuri instead of bringing it up like that? Boy, your moods! First, you brood at the dinner table as if we're planning a funeral instead of an engagement . . .Then, you hurl this Madhuri bombshell—"

I turned and looked at the clock: 1 AM.

"What did Ravi say? About Madhuri?" I asked.

Mina clicked her tongue. "He said nothing that you don't already know, I'm sure. But let me tell you one thing: if you meant to break us up, it hasn't worked—"

"Why would I want to do that?" I sat up in bed.

"I haven't a clue but you know something? I'm glad you brought up this Madhuri business. I've been doing a lot of thinking since Ravi left and I've come to the conclusion that the way he dealt with the situation was very decent. He actually offered to marry her. I mean, which college boy is willing to take that kind of responsibility? It's unfortunate that such a thing ever happened but now that I know it did—I don't really care. It's not as if he betrayed me or anything, because I didn't even know him then. His past is his past. It has nothing to do with our future."

I nodded. "It was never my intention to break the engagement. You must believe me, Mina. The truth is I don't know myself why I blurted out—"

"It doesn't matter," Mina interrupted. "But next time you get into one of your foul moods, think before you open your mouth . . . By the way, Ma told me about the mango tree."

"Ma told you. When?"

"After I came home this evening. Ma's been to that garden, Gita. Apparently there are almond trees there—" she said.

"But I'm sure this was a mango tree," I said.

"Oh, the one you were looking at undoubtedly was but Ma thinks your white-robed Huzoor must have been looking further into the garden. Ma says mango and almond trees are pretty similar. Almond is shorter, I think, but they both have small, pink blossoms—"

"Why didn't Ma tell me this herself?" I asked.

"Because you were in such a mood that you would have bitten her head off for disagreeing with you," Mina said. "But we'd better get some sleep. All of us are invited out to dinner tomorrow night—or should I say, tonight. To friends of Aunt Krishna's. Should be fun. Goodnight." Mina switched off my lamp.

She left my bedroom door open and no sooner had I closed my eyes than I saw sleep turn the corner, come running my way.

Chaya Bhuvaneswar

PENANCES

Hector Tuiz is beautiful. I've never been close to a face like his before. Nose slightly flat and hooked like Chac Zutz, the Mayan Lord of the Sun, in fierce profile. His eyes are shaped like a cat's, the colour of a jaguar or of sandstone lighter than his skin, and his lips are chapped and deep pink, soft and thick. Hector is Queche-Indian-brown, darker than me, and comes from Guatemala, where the national bird is the *quetzal*, which lives high in the blue-green and gold cloud forests of Alta Verapaz, and where there is a civil war, and where the Pacaya volcano, twenty-one miles outside Guatemala City and visible by plane on the flight from Miami, is an orange molten dump for the corpses of murdered Indian villagers. In 1864, canal workers digging near Puerto Barrios, on the Caribbean coast, found an apple-green jade plaque from the ancient city of Tikal; it was then stolen by Leiden, Amsterdam and even named the Leiden Plaque. But Hector's face is on that plaque, a Mayan warlord's face; triumphant, he carries a spear.

One Wednesday in 1981, Hector saw his last market day in Chichicastenanga, Chela for short. His mother and other Indian women from Chela and neighbouring villages had brought *chamarros* and *huipiles* they had woven on home-made looms, bright coloured clothes to catch the eye of white tourists. Hector took her there in the morning, drank some *atol*, and left for work. The women sold small earthenware pots, tortillas, and fragments of what they said were Indian arrowheads to wandering soldiers as well. Later that night, as Hector's mother folded up her wares, a *ladino* soldier came and raped her. Afterwards he gave her a bag of corn and told her to start a new life. Looking into her eyes, he muttered, "*Mas stupido que un indio*," tossing her his quartz, steel-plated watch and some money before walking away. Within days she had sold her two chickens, one pig, loom, Hector's bike, old TV set, and the bag of corn and the watch. She found a *quoyote* willing to take her and Hector to Mexico. Hector left his job at a *finca*, and within weeks they crossed over at San Cristobal huddled in the bottom of a banana truck owned by *El Pulpo*, American United Fruit Company, aka "Octopus."

At six o'clock promptly, every day, Hector reaches the building where my father lives. He cleans at night, thorough and unobtrusive. Few, if any, of the tenants would recognize him if they passed him on the street. But I did.

He was on his way uptown, resting on a bench at Park Avenue and Ninety-second Street, only three blocks away from the border of Spanish Harlem. It was a mild November day. He wore black low-slung jeans, a long-sleeved thermal under shirt, and a thin nylon navy blue jacket. He had his arms folded across his chest, relaxed. In the Mayan village of Socotz, Mexico, when children enter a hut to say good night or good morning to their parents, they stand with their arms folded like that, tips of their fingers under their forearms.

When I walked by Hector that day, on my way to hear a free Schubert lieder concert at Goethe House on Eighty-ninth and Fifth, he clicked his tongue to make me look at him. I remembered him at once and, without thinking, came over. "You must keep your distance from that kind," Appa has always said to me.

His eyes were amber in the light. He patted the space next to him on the bench, but I ignored that. "You do have pretty eyes," I said, "I'll see you around," swaying my hips as I walked away because I knew he was watching me.

The first time we met was at the service door of my father's building, which I had mistaken for the main entrance. The illuminated windows and fountain gleamed richly in the darkness. I decided to go inside and see if Appa was home, but when the glass door opened, only Hector was standing there. He looked me over, took me by the elbow and led me around to the grand front. He was amused. I went up in the elevator right away and tried Appa's door, but no one was home. Standing there and ringing the bell, I wondered if there was a woman, naked and soft, with burnt-sienna skin like the janitor's and smooth straight black hair, who was waiting for him to come home, smoking and lying on their bed and looking out of the window. Back in the elevator, I pressed L for "lobby" but it meant "lower level," and when the doors opened, Hector was there. He got in with his bucket and mop, looking skeptical, and asked, "You know someone who lives here?" My cheeks were burning. I pretended not to hear. He stepped closer.

"You got a problem with your ears?"

"My father lives here."

"What's his name?"

"I told the doorman. He let me in."

Defensive, I turned away from him and looked up at the floor numbers flashing yellow above the door. We were going up to ten, I saw with irritation. After he finally got out, I'd have to go all the way back down to the first floor. Suddenly he brushed my cheek with his forefinger. I flinched. "It's okay, it's just an eyelash," he said, showing me on his fingertip.

A few weeks later I saw him on that bench uptown, at the edge of the Park. So the next day I came to the building again, and the day after that, at six o'clock, when he gets there.

Mr Beech, my music teacher knows. It's April now and for five months I haven't been acting the same. You can't tell someone's a virgin from the way she walks or sits, but you can tell a lover from her breathlessness, flushed face, her indifference to you. At first he thought it was the excitement of winning a scholarship. Now he's guessed the truth, but wants to hear it from me. "It won't be easy for you to leave for Philadelphia, will it, Kalyani?" he asks. "You're quite popular here. Your parents must have to shoo away a lot of boys." Hector is nineteen, not a boy, and I am not popular. His lips that take mine between them, first moistened by my tongue tracing his smile and flicking inside his mouth, are the first lips I've ever kissed in my life. With Mr Beech I shake my head and ask politely, "Shall I do the Chausson for next time?" He'll try again. He's patient and imaginative.

But Appa has no idea.

In Guatemala, there's propaganda everywhere, printed-up lies for people who can read, symbols for those who can't. After centuries of *reducciones*, *encomienda* and *repartimiento* laws, through which the

Church and government gave Indian land to the Spaniards and then forced the Indians to work on it for free, there isn't enough arable land left for the small farmers. Indian men look for work in the lowlands, and people leave old places like Chajul and Nebaj to live in Guatemala City slums, *asentamientos*, which have been called "the belt of misery." Thousands of people live in garbage dumps because the bits of glass and paper they can find can be sold. In January 1984, a ten-year-old boy died under the wheels of an approaching dump truck while trying to retrieve a leftover Christmas wreath from a rotting pile of food.

Forced labour legally ended with the 1944 revolution, but the army still sweeps the Indian crowds at soccer games or Mayan festivals and forces conscriptions. The army is tough, *kaibil*, known to shoot a man for carrying a dozen tortillas in his hand, since that much food must be for the "subversives." In the Ixil Triangle, the widows and children tall enough to hold a hoe are made to work on "model villages," the army's idea, in which it lays down ten villages for every fifty they destroyed.

The Queche story of the Spanish conquerors says that when they came, they made a river of blood. The Spanish priests claimed to be shocked as the *conquistadores* "laid waste to all that was in their path, human and animal." But afterwards it was the Church that punished Mayan rituals, forcing the Indians to live within 560 yards of a church bell tower so they would hear the call to Mass. The Mayans went underground, worshipping in dark caves or *cenotes*, their ancient sources of water.

A Queche sacred book, the Popol Vuh, says that in the beginning of the world, when the gods created men of flesh and blood, they were so cruel to one another that the gods replaced them. But not all of them. In the first fifteen years of Spanish conquest, five million people were killed. Today, in just a few years of civil war, it is 500,000 people. Last December, General Meija Victores said, "Isn't the killing of a couple hundred Indians worth it to save the country?"

The day before my fifteenth birthday, over dinner at *Bukhara*, a fancy Indian restaurant not far from his building, I tell Appa some of these facts. He puts down his knife and fork (Never use your fingers in a restaurant! Too many Indians do that), dabs at his mouth with a napkin like an American (as he has taught me to do), and asks, with a bemused smile, "Kalyani, why do you care?"

I don't answer. It's a big concession, this dinner. I know he's told himself that it's the first step in bringing me into his "new life," showing me off, showing everyone that he didn't do anything wrong. *I have another daughter/Who I am sure is kind and comfortable.* He takes a sip of water and goes on. "Just be glad you don't live in a place like Gwadda-whatever, hah? You have a bright future here. You've won this prize to go study in Philadelphia, it'll help you. We'll do a special puja at the temple. Lakshmi puja. Then you'll get into a top college and get a good job afterwards. I'll do your taxes for free. You get in with a nice company, like IBM or GM. They'll take care of you. These days, even girls can study engineering if they want."

Appa has his plans. I have mine.

"Will you pay for Vidya to go to college, Appa?"

He gives a short laugh. "She won't need it."

O reason not the need! "You'll give her the money anyway?"

He smiles and shakes his head. In the candlelight he looks young, even flirtatious, his salt-and-pepper hair distinguished and neatly combed, his face merely tanned, rather than brown, above a charcoal-grey suit—as smooth and fit as a young Laurence Olivier, who, in their love scenes, refused to touch the Anglo-Indian, one-quarter-blackie actress Merle Oberon.

"You girls stick together, don't you?" he says. "Well, alright."

Every Easter, Hector says, you can see young and middle-aged *ladino* men in a procession during Holy Week. They strain under the load of heavy wooden andas, or floats, some of them half a block long and weighing as much as three tons. In a tradition brought long ago from Catholic Spain, they walk with laboured breaths through the streets of Guatemala City, paying for each promenade. Some keep on walking, round and round, until dawn the next day. Panting and grunting with exhaustion they attract the curious stares of Indian men and women who wash dishes and clean toilets at city hotels like the Camino Royale, watching the parade from back windows.

But each round the *ladinos* make with their floats costs fifty *quetzals*, more than an Indian will earn in two months. Only the wealthy can afford such penances.

A Ritual Exchange

GINU KAMANI

"We're running out of toilet paper," my mother muttered, handing over the one diminishing roll. The loosely rolled paper came free of the cardboard cylinder quite easily, so in handling it I had to be careful. We each knew whose period it was as the toilet roll migrated from bathroom to bathroom as needed. The paper was rough and erratically absorbent, locally produced and available only in pharmacies. Sometimes the paper was bluish, sometimes close to parcel brown. Sometimes the local pharmacy ran out and we had to wait several weeks. The roll had to be hand held as the bathrooms had no wall dispensers. The toilet paper was instituted after too many spots of blood fell to the tile between the commode and the basin and were left exposed in plain sight.

The toilet paper could not remain dry in those Indian bathrooms with just a few inches of wall separating the bathing area from the rest of the room. Water usually splashed everywhere, if not while showering then certainly during ayah's daily washing of our clothes. She soaked and sudsed and beat the fabrics with great vigour, drenching herself from head to toe. In those final moments when she wrung out the clothes, water flew through the air and covered every surface. She did not care for toilet paper, and could not be persuaded to ensure its dryness, so special little cabinets had to be installed in two of the three bathrooms to house the precious paper and, as was customary with all stored essentials, were fastened with large iron locks to ensure that the servants did not steal bits of it away. The key to this cupboard in our bathroom was the only house key assigned to us girls. All other keys stayed securely with our mother.

Around the house, goods of all kinds were stashed under lock and key. The wooden kitchen cabinets had the most locks, guarding essentials like sugar, salt, oil, flour, rice, wheat and dals. The glass cabinets in the pantry were packed with jars of chili-roasted peanuts, spiral *chaklees*, masala potato wafers; hidden away in the back gleamed the highly coveted foreign items: chocolates, peanut butter, processed cheese, corn flakes, cookies, spam.

The monthly feminine supplies were stored in my mother's wardrobe, a gray stainless steel monster with several racks for her saris, blouses, petticoats; odd-sized drawers for jewelry and knickknacks; and a locking safe for money. The bulky bags of sanitary towels were stuffed into the back of the narrow bottom shelf, and at the beginning of each period my sister Sunita and I were allowed to extract six days' worth of supplies, estimated at four pads per day for the first two, three pads a day for the next three, and two for the final day.

I had yet to come to terms with my period. The arrival of this monthly affliction became known to me in the most peculiar way. My father's last trip to Europe had led to a bountiful harvest of dark satin underwear —navy blue, chocolate brown and black. These undergarments were thrilling, and we showed them off proudly to our friends at school. On the annual school trip, an overnight stay at a hill resort near Bombay, we discovered that the rest house was home to many mice. They scampered out of drawers and cabinets, driving the girls into a frenzy. Divesting myself of the day's clothes before showering at night, I left them in a heap near my bag. In the morning, as we rushed to pack for the return, I scooped my clothes off the floor and noticed a gaping hole in my panties. On closer examination it became clear that the entire crotch area was missing.

I was ten years old and acutely embarrassed. I hid the underwear deep inside my bag. I did not comprehend until later that the rats had eaten out the fabric, having lucked upon a tasty morsel. It was only on awakening at home the next morning with stains on the back of my nightie that I realized my period had begun. Only then did I display the chewed-up underwear to my mother, who laughed aloud as she divined the chain of events, congratulating the rats in their choice of dessert.

That early restrained spotting was the last time the bleeding announced itself daintily. From then on, my chum always arrived with gushing force, and the exasperated ayah was forever having to clean up after me.

I hated this part of "growing up." My body had changed right under me without my authority. I was outfitted with a full new internal wardrobe: plasticized panties, elastic belt, sanitary napkins to sling between my legs; and of course enjoined to partake of the precious toilet paper, which kept the blood off the tile. However, the thrill of having regular access to a commodity as expensive as toilet paper soon became an adequate reward for harbouring the monthly succubus. Particularly because this access was strictly reserved for the girls.

My brother Prashant complained vigorously about this rule. Anything denied him was a victory for his sisters, and he hated that. When asked what he intended to do with the toilet paper, he replied that he would start a collection, which he could add to his box of shiny chocolate foils. Prashant was a master collector. Besides the metallic foils, he collected matchboxes, cocktail stirrers, coins, colour pencils, erasers and comic books. Now he wanted bits of the variously tinted rolls of toilet paper, making a fuss every time the medical store sent up a delivery. "Compared to chocolate, toilet paper is expensive!" fumed my mother, crushing his hopes completely.

One day while cleaning out Prashant's desk, my mother found a neat pile of paper squares hidden in the bottom of a box of cards. On closer examination she recognized them as sections of toilet paper. Immediately she accused Sunita and me of carelessness and threatened to deduct the cost out of our pocket money. We protested that we had done no wrong, that he must have stolen it. She made sure the bathroom cabinets were securely locked, counted the squares of paper in my brother's desk, then waited a while. Prashant was an inveterate hoarder. Anything he embarked on accumulating, he had to increase continually, no matter the amount already in possession. A few days later when my mother checked, the number of toilet paper squares had indeed increased. She was incensed. That evening, when my brother returned from school, she caught him by the ear and slapped him in front of everyone, accusing him of stealing. Humiliated by the blow, he screamed that he had collected it on his own and it was no one else's business where he got it.

What did he do with it? my mother inquired suspiciously, at which my brother's face turned red and his lips sealed shut. This clear indication of guilt earned him another hard slap and banishment to his room. Try as my mother might, he refused to divulge his source, knowing rightly that she would humiliate the offender. Rummaging through his waste basket she found that the wadded balls of tissue concealed the sticky mucous of his nightly revelry. Searching through his clothes my mother discovered cheap American paperbacks with miniskirted blondes gracing the covers. I remember thinking it peculiar that Prashant read books about girls, since he assiduously avoided females in all forms.

The idea that my brother was wasting some poor soul's hard-earned money gave my mother intense anxiety. The thin pile of neat white squares rested on her desk. She stared at it periodically as she went about the house. Finally it struck her that the paper was of a vastly superior quality compared to our locally available brands. She had me confirm that in fact the paper was soft and absorbent and definitely not manufactured in India. This confounded us even further. Where would a schoolboy find imported toilet paper? This quality of toilet roll was only available in the Smugglers' Market, for five times the usual price. Back went my mother to threaten my brother, this time whacking him solidly across the bottom. At fourteen, this was rather insulting for him, and he steeled himself with angry resolve. Grounded at home for a full week, he still refused to confess. The servants and driver provided no clues. Our closest cousins revealed no confidence. Mothers of his friends were equally ignorant.

Motivated by promises of imported Kit Kat normally rationed out only on birthdays, my sister and I took to spying on Prashant. Since we lived in a Bombay high-rise with no garden or greenery close by, children generally gathered in the game room in the basement to play table tennis or billiards, or in the spacious lobby where the indulgent homeowners' association permitted roller-skating, hide-and-seek, gossiping, and wrestling.

When the boys played round-robins of table tennis, a group of us girls concentrated on knocking about billiard balls on the green felt.

When they played football in the lobby, we wheeled around on our roller skates. When they gathered around the watchman's radio to listen to cricket matches, we settled on the floor to play five stones. As we had always suspected, the activities of boys were extremely dull, and our friends quickly bored of our much hyped espionage and went their separate ways. My sister and I took to organizing our stamp collection, diligently pasting new arrivals into our album. Almost everyday there were letters from relatives in the US, so we constantly fussed over the American section.

One evening an Ambassador car unloaded its passengers at the front. From one side stepped Mr and Mrs Chopra, who lived on the fourth floor, and from the other side emerged a blond giant. His hair was long and curled around his ears, and he wore jeans and a t-shirt. The boys were spread over the lobby playing mock cricket with rolled-up newspaper and a foam ball, but paused to allow the residents through the passage. The blond giant raised his hand in greeting, and when we followed his gaze, much to our astonishment, he was waving at our brother, suddenly puffed up like a peacock and brazenly waving back. We were instantly jealous. Our heads were still turned when the firangi suddenly leaned over us, admiring our American stamps.

"Hiya!" he said jovially, causing us to jump in fright. "You like stamps? I've got a ton of those. Come over any time—flat 42. See ya." He waved and slouched off as Mr Chopra held the lift door open for him.

We were shocked. Had he really spoken to us? We looked around to make sure we weren't dreaming. The boys were standing around dumbstruck by this exchange, so we knew it must have been real. The thought of tapping into a bottomless source of stamps sent us into a frenzy. Our pouting brother was all but forgotten. Sunita and I raced up seven flights of stairs to our apartment, too impatient to await the return of the elevator. We leaned on the door bell until the harassed cook came muttering to unlock the door. We shouted aloud for our mother.

"Memsahib is out," he snapped. "And Daddy?" we demanded. The cook pointed to the master bedroom. Dad always left a trail to mark his passage through the house. First, his briefcase in the hall. Then, his tie draped around a door knob. A few feet further, the kicked-off shoes. And finally the man himself, reclining in a leather armchair with whiskey-soda and masala peanuts close at hand.

He smiled at us through tired eyes, and we draped ourselves over his shoulders, begging for permission to meet the American. Dad had actually heard about this blond exchange student, as he often ran into Mr Chopra at the club. He had misgivings about two young girls going to visit an older boy, but when we mentioned the offer of American stamps, he nodded sympathetically and gave his consent, as long as the ayah went with us.

We went in search of our servant. She was temperamental and stubborn. We needed a way to entice her, since she would have to interrupt some important chore to accompany us. The Chopras lived in 42. Down the hall in 44, the Modi family employed a girl who was from our ayah's village. After escorting us to the Chopras, she could easily slip out the servant's entrance and go visit her friend. The deal was struck and we rushed down the stairs, urging the maid along.

The Chopras had one of the largest flats in the building, having combined two units. Both their sons were away at college, so the American student had no company his own age. The servant let us in and motioned to one of the bedrooms. My sister and I drew deep breaths to force down the excitement hammering at our chests. We rapped lightly on the door.

"Come in!" sang the foreign voice and we entered cautiously. He sat at his desk, doing homework. Even as he wrote, his fountain pen ran dry and he shook it furiously. A spurt of ink flew across the room and landed on the wall.

"Oh shit!" he muttered, scrambling to his feet. Using the side of his palm, he swiped at the ink, then dabbed at the stain with saliva and a handkerchief. "I hate these damn things," he sighed, tossing the gold-nibbed pen into the waste basket. "I know they don't allow pencils, but they'll just have to make an exception for me!" He spun a pencil high into the air and caught it behind his back. In that brief moment my sister and I both noted that it was a foreign pencil, with a pink rubber eraser on the end. We were practically licking our lips when he turned to us with a greeting.

"Hi, I'm Jim!" he announced, and thrust his hand out to be shaken. Unaccustomed to shaking hands, we stood as we were and stared at him in silence. "Sorry!" he apologized, putting his hands in his pockets.

"Have a seat," he gestured at his unmade bed, the sheets rumpled and uncovered. "I'm Jim," he prompted again, and we nodded to indicate our comprehension. Accustomed only to direct questions like "What's your name?" we didn't reciprocate with an answer.

Jim chatted on, unperturbed by our shyness. He had come for a year as a senior exchange student from some place in Ohio. He thought Bombay was "real cool, a real trip." He loved the crowds—"never seen so many people hangin' around." The girls were "real cute." "Couldn't get a date, no way, though." There was one other exchange student at the school with him, a kid from Poland, and both were exempt from wearing the mandatory school uniform. That made the Indian kids "real mad," and that was "cool."

My sister and I sat transfixed. Here was a character straight out of the movies, a hippie-looking kid who spoke real American slang. He pulled out a pack of cigarettes, flipped up the top and offered them to us. My sister and I started giggling then, and couldn't stop. We pressed our hands tightly over our mouths to contain the burbling while Jim lit up. I spotted the stack of letters on the bedside table and reached for them.

"Oh yeah, stamps!" he laughed, carefully tearing the corners off each envelope and placing them into our outstretched hands. "You be sure and share, you hear? No fighting. Hey, you got any older sisters?" He gathered up the letters and slid them into the desk drawer. I caught a glimpse of more white stationery in the depths, and was finally moved to speak.

"Don't you have any more?" I inquired eagerly, pointing to the back of the drawer. Jim bent down and looked. "Good eyes," he congratulated, and pulled out two more stacks. My sister fidgeted on the bed in excitement. This was a gold mine. Our friends would be very jealous. Even our brother would be irritated. Oh! Prashant . . .

"Are you a friend of my brother?" I asked Jim, who shrugged and asked his name. I told him. Jim thought for a moment. "Skinny guy, glasses, plays ping-pong real good?" we nodded. "Yeah, I know him. I call him Shanty. Real cool cat."

"He's not cool, he's stupid!" retorted my sister, incensed that Prashant could be lavished with such praise. "He's a bully, and tells lies, and Mummy is very angry with him."

"Oh yeah?" Jim continued tearing stamps off the letters. "All I know is, I needed some quick cash and he obliged by buying some books off of me. Worked out for both of us, yessirree." My sister and I exchanged looks of alarm.

"Oh, so that's where he—" spluttered Sunita. I cut her off quickly.

"Do you know lots of people, Jim? You're very lucky to get so many letters. Can you find pen pals for our friends? I bet Sunita wants one too, don't you?" I nudged my sister in the ribs and she drew back in irritation.

"Well," said Jim, cocking an eyebrow. "Seems like you have tongues after all!"

From then on we visited Jim every few days to check for newly arrived mail. My mother's concern about our being alone with him vanished when we confirmed him as the source of Prashant's paperbacks. We begged for more time to see what else we could discover.

Jim's list of buddies yielded pen pal opportunities for all our friends. We knew the letters took up to two weeks in the mail each way, so we waited patiently for replies. The monsoon finally arrived and with it the usual floods, school closings and deliciously cool temperatures. The rain also brought seasonal illnesses, and we soon received word that Jim had developed jaundice.

Our entire family went down to commiserate. The Chopras were very nervous, and had even rung up Jim's parents in the States. Even though their household was vegetarian, Mrs Chopra ordered chicken and fish broth prepared as supplements to the invalid's liquid diet. After repeated warnings against disturbing him, Prashant, Sunita and I quietly entered Jim's room. He was dozing in bed, a book by Mickey Spillane on his chest. Prashant lurched toward the book but then stepped back quickly when he realized we were watching. Sunita and I looked over the desk for new letters. Prashant slipped into Jim's bathroom and locked the door behind him. I beckoned Sunita and we bent down to look through the key hole. Prashant reached into the mirrored cabinet and pulled out a white roll. Toilet paper! He carefully detached several squares, folding them neatly and dividing them between his trouser pockets.

I hurried to Jim's bed and woke him. He frowned at the sight of

Sunita and myself bending over him. I whispered urgently that Prashant was stealing his toilet paper. He blinked uncomprehendingly. I repeated that Prashant had locked himself in the bathroom and was stealing sheets from the toilet roll! Jim smiled weakly, his jaundiced eyes twinkling. He pointed to a suitcase stored high up on a shelf over the door.

"The whole bag's full of it!" he laughed. "You can all help yourselves. No sweat." I looked up at the suitcase in awe. "The whole bag?" I echoed in disbelief. "Yeah, sure," he continued. "I was told I'd never find toilet paper in India, so I brought my own, enough for a year. 'Course there's no dispenser, so I usually keep one roll on top of the toilet, but Mrs C always stuffs it into the cabinet, 'cause that old biddy who cleans the place sure loves to splash that water around."

At that very moment, I felt a sudden rush of liquid between my legs and realized to my horror that my period had arrived and blood was gushing through my crotch. Without even looking I knew I'd made a mess. I could only imagine how bad. I felt my cheeks blazing with embarrassment. I stood up nonchalantly and stole a quick glance at the sheet. There was a sizable stain. Tears gathered in my eyes as I silently motioned to Sunita to cover up the blotch. Her face twisted in horror but she moved over so her dress concealed it. I hurried to the bathroom door and banged on it, shouting at Prashant to get out. He flushed the toilet and unlocked the door, his pockets bulging. I ran in and turned the lock, snatched some toilet paper from the cabinet and stuffed it into the key hole. Then I wadded up the remainder of the toilet roll and shaped it into a pad, packing it into my damp underwear. When I stepped out, Prashant was gone, the bedroom door was closed and Sunita was standing over the now open suitcase, confronting a sea of toilet rolls, stacked three deep in the spacious bag.

"You weren't supposed to get up!" I hissed at Sunita. She did not respond, lovingly caressing each blinding white roll.

When I turned to Jim, he was intently fingering the blood stain on his sheet. "I'm sorry," I mumbled, burning up once again. "Please don't tell anyone. I'll call the servant and she'll change the sheet right away."

"What?" Jim looked up, beaming. "Don't you worry your pretty li'l head about it. I'm not mad," he assured me. He had a strange look on his face. "Look," he added, "you like that toilet paper? Huh? You want it? Take it, okay, it's yours. It's about time I learned how to rinse my butt with water."

We heard his words, but could not comprehend them. An entire suitcase full of toilet paper was an unimaginable generosity. We were speechless.

"No, seriously, take it. It's yours. Just return the suitcase. And . . . don't worry about the sheet. I'll take care of it." He stroked the stain once more, a sideways smile tugging at his lips. He lifted the edge clear off the bed and held it to the light. The blood was a dark ruby on the snowy white sheet. He gave a low whistle of appreciation. "It's a beauty!" he whispered in awe. He struggled off the bed and pried the sheet free of the mattress. Folding rapidly, he bundled it into the desk then lay down again with the blanket over him.

Without further ado, my sister and I snapped the suitcase shut and gripped the handle together. We opened the door and breathlessly took our leave. In full view of the chatting adults outside we raced out of the front door and up the stairs to our flat. We hauled the bag to our bedroom and stuffed as many rolls as we could into our wardrobe, behind the piles of party outfits stored in tall muslin-wrapped bundles. We each managed to squash ten rolls into the back. That left at least thirty rolls for our mother. We rushed the bag to our parents' bedroom with barely a moment to spare as Mummy came charging in wondering what nonsense we were up to.

"Ssssshhh!" we cautioned her, pointing to the bag meaningfully.

"What's in it?" she demanded.

"Look, look!" we offered generously.

She unlocked the bag and opened it impatiently. The sight of the tightly-wound fat rolls of tissue knocked the wind out of her and she collapsed onto the bed. Her lips quivered with excitement as she hugged us both to her. "Oh my god, there's enough in here for five years!" she shrieked. Sunita and I linked arms around her middle, reaching for the cluster of keys hooked into her waist. We located the key to the chocolate cupboard and dangled it in front of her face. "Go, go, go!" she motioned us out, and set about counting her treasure.

Everyone in the house recognized the sound of the chocolate cupboard being unlocked and opened. Prashant came tearing in to the pantry. We held up the master keys for his inspection. His face fell. His brow blackened with outrage.

"How did you get those keys?" he screamed. "Give them to me or I'll tell Mummy right now!" We stuck our tongues out and made farting noises.

"Go tell," we shouted triumphantly, pulling out bar after bar of Kit Kat. Prashant was paralyzed with dismay.

"It's not fair!" he howled, stamping his feet. "Give me some," he grabbed at our hands.

"What's in your pocket, Prashant?" I pointed at the indiscreet lumps. He backed off, sulking.

"We know where the toilet paper came from, so you better shut up. If you don't want us to tell Mummy you stole it from Jim, you better give us your pocket money for the next six months."

Prashant's legs wobbled uncertainly and then he sank back against the counter. "You spied on me," he whispered, stunned. He scowled in preparation for an angry follow-up but then thought better of it and hung his head. The Kit Kat crunched pleasantly in our mouths. "But . . . but . . . six months is too much. That's sixty rupees. Take three months, okay? Or I won't be able to buy any table tennis balls." Prashant pleaded with folded hands. Revenge was certainly sweet.

"Tell you what—you give us all the books you're hiding, and give us this month's pocket money now. Tomorrow, ask your friends to collect any stamps they can get. Promise? Swear on god." Prashant pinched the skin of his neck and swore on the code of childhood honour. Then he fished the ten-rupee note out of his shirt and handed it over coolly. Cool cat, Jim had anointed him.

"You better empty your pockets quickly because she's definitely going to search you today." Prashant pulled out the wads of paper, then looked around uncertainly for a disposal site.

"Here, you take it," he thrust both hands at me.

I snatched it from him, then reached into my underwear and stuffed the paper inside. "Thanks. I really needed that." Prashant turned beet red with shame.

"You've gone mad!" he screeched, his cries bouncing off the walls as he ran through the kitchen and into his room, bolting the door solidly behind him. Cool cat indeed.

Beloved

AUSMA ZEHANAT KHAN

I am wearing a ring on my finger that doesn't belong. My mother never wore a ring, it was never part of her tradition. The diamonds are beautiful, sparkling, but they are cold as well. Not a lamp within a glass like a shining star. Nothing to illuminate the heavens and the earth. Or me. Just angles and refraction, coal pressed and suffered into perfection. But if it was from you—

I am branded. A possession that turns on the shy edge of a smile and on the glinting angle of a stone without soul. The lack of connection is soul-deep, expanding into every corner of my consciousness. With every faculty, every hard-won breath of self, I know my incompleteness. I know that this was not the name written in the stars for the wind to swallow whole. Seed in the earth sprouting into a circle around a finger on my hand. My skin, bit by bit, creeps away from this ownership and familiar territory becomes foreign. Whose veins are beating with blood's rhythm? Whose breath is pale and hesitant? I do not know the truth and strangeness of her existence. She is a foreigner, too. She speaks an unspeakable language and wears a stranger's mask.

My thoughts are all for your dark eyes and fleeting smile. This is where my real self resides, longing and longing. Warm and free like a breeze released from the deep recesses of a stifled earth. A blanket has been spread over the ground and the grass suffocates. You look or don't look and I go on each day feeling the band of gold get tighter and the edge of the stones get sharper.

I wish to consecrate myself to you, but a veil comes down and separates the self that belongs from the self that resides nowhere. I am new with new colours, new words. I lose the direction I was walking in. When I wake, I don't think and I don't break. I have the strength of ancestors and I bear their weight upon my finger.

It is a satisfactory arrangement.

*

Ami is buying my jewelry today, though I told her I would wear what my grandfather gave her. There is a necklace with three golden chains, which matches the golden triangle I will wear on the side of my hair. This is enough, I tell her, enough. I don't need more, we just don't have the money. But she tells me it is expected, their eyes will dwell on my neck to see how precious I was to my father.

Links of gold to form a chain to bind my ankles together. Ami, won't he love me? Won't he look at my smile and the sun on my hair and love me? Or will he build his understanding of me from the pressure cookers and coffee pots you give me? He should see the beautiful word in the simple line of a singing poem. He should listen to it breathe and learn my secrets through its syllables.

He doesn't want to know me. He wants to marry me. I want to walk away, shed my traditions like a skin that cloaks and chokes, start fresh from a naked essence unknown.

But every word will betray. Some traitor will walk down the stairs to the kitchen to see if the henna has settled in the fridge. She will open the door and the neighbours will smile their goodwill into the cupboards where garlands are stored. So much is cooking on the stove and what is the bride doing downstairs? I wanted to see if my *mehndi* was ready. Look at her, she's not shy at all, they laugh. Have you ever known a bride so eager to have her hands painted? I wanted to see the patterns, so I could decide. Decide what? Everything is ready, everyone is ready but you. Go upstairs and rest.

But there's music playing in the family room and everybody is singing along. Always, always I think of you.

The present they have brought me is so beautiful. Almost it understands me. A set of silver pens because she likes to write. He didn't come with them, so who will free the words? I want to talk to the stranger, want to say his name, and feel if it resonates inside my heart. But he doesn't come as they feed me sweets and wipe the lipstick off the paleness of my cheek.

She isn't eating. I think she's just nervous, *Ami* says. Nothing to be nervous about. Not tonight. Bawdy humour around the room, and she sits there quietly, wondering who moved the Quran into the other room. Look at her pretending she doesn't know what we're talking about. More laughter. I don't know. I don't know him.

All he talks about night and day is her, what she likes, where he wants to take her. She isn't responding, they don't expect that. She sits still and silent, pale marble cold, her eyes fixed on the flower garlands round her ankles. His mother pats her hair, fixing her veil so her neck will not show as much. I like a simple girl and I am simple. But he doesn't understand. Is he nervous? No, no. He's laughing and talking, he struts when he walks down the street. But sometimes I see him looking into the mirror as if he isn't sure what he sees.

I look up. *Ami*, is it true? Is he wondering how I'll see him?

I know what you are thinking. I am wearing a ring that represents surrender. I see my reflection in its blank, white surfaces. Your indifference has made me into a thing steely and cold, a thing that accepts and is defined by rules that follow an empty tradition. Your golden arrow pierced me through and through. But I can do this. I can do this.

The clean angles of your cheekbones repudiate. If you frown and turn away you judge the lesser against the greater and you judge falsely. I am blind and I wear tattered clothing but my hunger for knowledge is so great. I am devout in my desire to do service to you.

Always, always I think of you. I wish they would turn that song off. They don't know what it means to me and when I try to tell them, you disappear into the shadows of the surface. There is beauty in the words you speak but what transfixes me is the courage in your eyes. Caught once, caught twice, each time looking deeper and finding there is enough there on the pale and sandy shore to spare support for me. The waves thunder across my realization and I am a blind devotee.

The *jhumr* is caught in my hair as they try to set it. I long, long for a language to form a chain to connect us at the level of soul, spirit, *ruh*.

I chase illusions from eyes and find myself facing the future in the cool surfaces of a silent diamond.

Why don't you cut off the past with a clean blade and let me build a future honed on compromises? There is no magic allegory in your eyes. The shadow of your smile is an ache inside me. I will go—go—go beyond, but there must be someone there to catch me.

Your indifference was an abdication. So now judge nothing as I put out my hand for a ring that I will end up wearing as a collar.

It is a barren form. And I am barren too.

We have ordered the *mithai* for the wedding today. It seems that the mouths of all those whom I love will be sweetened by the sharp taste of my defeat. Once I am cold it will no longer matter. I will become a reflection on a ring.

Put this silver over the *burfi*, it has no taste, but it looks pretty. We shouldn't be doing this on the wedding day, we should have done it yesterday. Your father forgot to order it. Cut it into heart shapes. You should have gotten her a cake, she always wanted a wedding cake in tiers. It's not our tradition. I don't like this foolish Western showmanship. Will the guests eat the cake? I don't think so. See. Then cut the *burfi*. Cut it into heart shapes and put the silver foil on it. It has no taste and it looks so pretty.

Are you listening as I tell you these details which mean my surrender? Won't you look at me and see danger? Won't you give me your name, in which I might find protection? Leaning and leaning and leaning until I fall right down.

That's now how I'm supposed to be. You were supposed to be my partner, not my crutch. You were supposed to love me. We were meant to walk towards each other. Foreigner. I loved you outside my limits. I can bear anything, everything, because I am so cold. But I can't sit here, pale and fragile, while you sample the *mithai*.

He chose a cream wedding dress for me, but I couldn't wear it. Not when you told me it was the colour you wanted to see me married in. Wear it, *beti*, he likes this colour for you. Think how pretty it will look against your hair. But she is a fair girl. Fair girls look their best in red. My son doesn't say much, you know. He's very shy. But he asked me to ask you to wear this colour for him. It's a colour he likes.

I was going to wear red like my mother. I wanted to be her special daughter, the daughter most like her. I had planned it before I even knew I wanted to be married. But you liked simplicity and I sold my dreams for a corner of your smile. I'll wear it, I promised you. I'll wear whatever colour you like. We can elope, I thought. I wanted to.

No men are allowed in here. No one's supposed to see the bride. I know you went to school together but that doesn't entitle you to be here now. You can congratulate her afterwards.

What were you looking at, beloved? The golden wedding dress? Or the empty places in my heart? I want to love. I want to spend this wealth of love that I've accumulated on you. I want to give myself on a level that eclipses all other giving, all other knowing, all other loving. I will take nothing but the look in your dark eyes and the pale shadow of your smile that causes music and torment in my heart. You are so alien and yet so known. So safe. Mists of my belonging, here stand I.

I will wear gold and cream, but I will not be wearing it for you. The veil has set over my jewelry, my face. As I sit beside him *Ami* places the mirror on my lap. I look like a porcelain doll, my features sculpted into a single day's cosmetic perfection. The curls I have never bothered with scroll onto my forehead. He's looking into the mirror to see his bride. Look up, everyone says. Everyone is teasing. Look up, he wants to drown in your eyes. But I won't open my eyes because the vision in the glass could shatter my heart. I could shatter him with the things I'm not saying. Beloved, beloved, it's too late. I completed the cycle of love. He's taking my hand and my fingers tremble in his grasp. There's a new circle, a new tradition. A new chain that binds us together as I sit there quiet and poised, never meeting his eyes.

Stranger. I must be happy with you. Such a beautiful match, such a beautiful match. She'll bring laughter into your house. She'll bring music. When this girl was growing up, there wasn't a day when we could get her to stop singing. She always told us she was going to save the world, and we told her that she'd marry a wonderful man and make him very happy. How do you feel, how do you feel? What do you think of your new bride, what's the verdict? She's nice. She's like ice and she won't melt.

A wild hot wind was blowing over my senses, I drank it as thirstily as a bird who hasn't flown in years. I stripped myself bare of everything, left only with the one word, the changing word, the teaching, living word. It was about surrender, this self-discovery. It wasn't about peace.

Who would have known that a word you were taught to worship all your life would one day descend like the razor edge of a crescent into your heart. They should have taught me to be gracious with my sacrifices, not cold, like marble. They should have said that the marriage isn't over when the gold is on your finger. Stranger. You chose gold for a girl who wanted to shake off her skin and she honours your choices as she will honour you. Now this is the only way to survive, to hold onto everything but myself.

It will be its own kind of freedom, losing all responsibility for my thoughts and my actions. Free in stasis. It couldn't be like that, could it? If I meet his eyes, will love for him flood my soul and lift me higher? Will I find him somehow, stumbling through the waves of self-rejection? Or will he look into my eyes and laugh at my songs like the rest. Except you. Except you, beloved.

I am twice betrayed. By my conscience and my longings. Your name is heavy on my heart. I want to meet you on the plane of the one word we share. Why can't some transcendental language sustain us? In loving you, I am worshipping. But a traitor walks down the stairs to the kitchen to decorate the hands that won't hold yours. I have betrayed nothing and yet my every glance gives secrets away. If you see me sitting there in cream, veiled and weighted down by *Ami's* jewelry, will you wish that you had spoken? I have broken my own traditions, but I have never broken my vows.

I wanted to fly, brave and beautiful, straight into your arms. I wanted to taste the words from your lips and find my own sweetness within them. I thought we named courage the same word in the same language. I whispered a word to you, you whispered back that its meaning had changed, there was nothing for me to anchor my hopes on. You have ended our communication and no one speaks to me any more. There is no freedom to say the word. It was stolen from me by your foreignness. Why were you constructed differently when we are the same? I see your beauty in any colour, wearing any banner, by any nationality you choose or discard. I see my belonging to you balanced on the edge of a perfect word. But the word has shattered like a pale sky torn away. It leaves me empty.

*

I am being decorated. My hands, my face, even my heart. The henna is orange and fragrant. I don't know if it moves me more or the girl who applies it with her gentle dedication. Her hair is dark like yours and I wonder if she will come to the same point of decision I am at. She could ask me for help but all I would be able to give her are betrayals. I was true to nothing. I am belled and glistening. A bride wearing gold not red, betraying each colour she thinks of.

She plays the bride so well, come on, smile. No one said you couldn't smile. Look at him sneaking glances in the mirror to see you. Give him a break, *beti*, look at him, don't be shy. They have their whole lives, to look at each other. The sweetest bride is the one who is shy, who doesn't look. People are congratulating her, she should look up and thank them. Oh, these are stupid traditions. If she wants to smile, she'll smile.

I am a bride with flower garlands and I have married a stranger. If I raise my eyes, it will not be to him but to you. I will meet your eyes and it is you that my coldness will salute. Beloved. Can you do something to pull me back? I'm losing myself, gold and marble. Nothing of me breathes anymore. I can't sing for you.

He puts another ring on my finger. His hands tremble on my veil, he is nervous. I could laugh or smile, ease his worry or confusion. But I will let him be what he is while I search for you in memories and songs. You put meaning in a single word with a glance from your dark, dark eyes. Why did you come to the wedding? Was it to watch me bleed or to confirm for yourself how little courage I truly had? If you come up to shake his hand and smile at me politely, I will break, and lie in pieces at your feet.

Ami is worried looking at you. At last, at last, does she understand the source of my confusion? Has she looked at you too late and seen? My God, *I should have let her marry him.* The stranger is anxious, you are looking too long at my neck. What are you doing? Go home and let me live in peace. There are people waiting behind you. Go away.

Beloved, don't look at me that way. I didn't want any of this. Don't memorize me as a bride of golden traditions. You will forget too quickly who I am. You will convince yourself I never spoke your language, never touched the softness of your curls, never drank the beauty of your eyes. This is a porcelain doll.

The stranger's knuckles are white in the mirror. What would you have me do?

Who is this man? A friend from school? What kind of friends has she been making? My son will not let this continue in the future. I don't know how she's been brought up. This is nothing to worry about. Girls go away to school all the time. I've never agreed with it, you let them study too much and their ideas become strange. Besides, living away from your parents' home—where does it say in the Quran you can do that? Someone tell this man to leave. He's not my guest. I didn't invite him.

Won't you go? What are you waiting for? I'm sorry, I'm sorry. He isn't feeling well. Can someone get him a glass of water? Oh my God, he's falling, someone catch him!

What kind of a bride is this? She won't look at my son and now she has her arms around some strange man who's not even Pakistani? I knew nothing good could come of sending her there. How did you raise this girl? Oh Lord, did you see that, she's taken her *dupatta* off!

Please, please, it's all right. He just needs a little air, he needs some room to breathe.

Will you sit down and behave yourself?

I can't. He isn't well.

He's not your husband!

Ami is crying as the stranger takes me away. This is a *rukhsati* the city won't forget. You didn't come to wish me well. I don't know why you came. My husband and I walk out to the car, under the Quran and smiles and whispers. The shameless bride doesn't cry. They open the car door for her to take her away and she stops. No one's heart beats faster. She has the ring upon her finger and a diamond in her soul.

I turn back, lost for words. You have extinguished the world with a look from your eyes, the haunting shadow of your smile. I turn back. I look up. I look at you. Then I walk away.

The Cat Who Cried

SHAUNA SINGH BALDWIN

She stood framed by the doorway with the hall lights blazing behind her, grey hair straggling from under her sari palloo, and Prem and I started up in bed, hearts thudding.

"The children?"

"Are you sick?"

"No, no. Worse than that." Maybe my Hindi is fading a little every year; I find it more and more difficult to understand her without her dentures.

"Then what happened?" asked Prem.

"I heard a cat crying outside."

I glanced at the window. Snow gusts swirled over the peaked roofs of the subdivision. Strange how sloping roofs are more familiar to me now than the hot shimmer-haze concrete flatness of an Indian city view.

"Mataji, you must have imagined it," Prem began, but I knew it would do not good.

"It's bad luck. Come, we must do puja. No one will ever say I allowed bad luck to come into this home."

Mataji's life has been dedicated to the collection of strategies to outwit bad luck and Prem knew it, so he stifled a yawn and a groan and led the way down to the drawing room—I mean the living room—collecting little Nikhil and his blanket from Mataji's bed and leaving baby Sheila sleeping.

We had no furniture in the living room, then. Just a large wool dhurrie we've moved to every place we've ever lived since we came to America and cushions of all colours and shapes and sizes. We bought the house because we wanted a crackling fire in the fireplace, but that would have to wait till Mataji returned to India because she'd made it her shrine, filling it with statues of Shiva and Ganesh and Vishnudevi, flowers and garlands, incense and Christmas tinsel. It was her refuge, where she began at five every morning to confide her irritation with twanging nasal syllables, the whiteness of people and the greyness of that twilight that arrived just when she was ready to face another day of strangeness.

"Mommy, what's Mataji doing?" Nikhil asked in English.

"A little puja, darling," I said, as brightly as I could.

"Don't tell him why," whispered Prem.

But I couldn't resist.

"Mataji heard a kitty crying," I said smiling sweetly at Prem. Then, remembering it's a wife's duty to keep peace, I lied. "So we're going to pray for it."

Prem sat next to Mataji as she began slowly and deliberately to recite the thousand names of Vishnu. Outside, church bells rang to call people to Midnight Mass and Mataji's bad luck cat stayed silent. I wanted to lift myself upwards and follow the sandalwood incense curling out of our chimney.

*

Mataji was suspicious of me as soon as she heard that her youngest son wanted to marry a woman he had met studying in America. That I am Indian was merely an indication of his good sense. That my parents sent their daughter to study in America was an indication of a family tendency towards wasteful spending. Mataji must have vowed to watch this trait closely for fear it should be passed along any further in her house, for as soon as we were married—in India, with all the appropriate ceremony—she made it clear that I was not to be trusted with money. Within two years, then, we had none left. My dowry distributed to Prem's family—all of whom blessed us enthusiastically—and with Prem unable to find a job where he did not have to give or take bribes to survive, we finally asked his brothers to sponsor us to America.

Mataji had been convinced ever since that I was a bad influence on the son who was to have lived with her in that huge white bungalow on Aurangzeb Road in her old age. When we decided not to have children till we could afford them, Prem began receiving piteous supplications to allow her to know her unborn grandchildren before she died and warnings that he must not be influenced by his over-educated wife. Like his three older brothers, Prem is unlikely to be influenced by anyone, least of all a woman, but he loves being the prize in a contest.

We didn't have children immediately. Instead we savoured the time to be just two of us exploring a new land, freed from obedience to Duty, awed by the power and burden of this thing called Choice, collapsing every night exhausted by endless everyday decisions, decisions, decisions. Prem got a job selling health and life insurance to other expatriate Indians—exiles, he calls them.

Prem is less adaptable than I; he has had much less practice. A few years ago he would have returned to India where there wouldn't be so many choices, but I quickly decided it was time to have children. Mataji came to visit us for the first time when my son Nikhil was born. And ever since, she spends six months of the year visiting each brother in turn.

Usually, she comes to visit in the summer to escape the Delhi heat, the loneliness, the power cuts and the water shortages, but this time she arrived in December, wrinkling her nose as she held her sari pleats high over the grey-black slush and yanking her precious bag with its tape recorder and bhajan cassettes out of the dark hands of a helpful old porter. She unpacked quickly and we gave her a glass of sherry in a tumbler that made it look sufficiently medicinal, and then she started her assault on Prem, speaking in English, which she believes makes us pay greater attention.

"I have decided to leave the house on Aurangzeb Road to you when I die," she said.

"Mataji, that is very kind and you can do as you wish, but you know we are four brothers and no one should get more than others."

"No, I have decided. Your father left me this house—that was his gift. I can give it to whom I like. But I have only one condition. You and she," gesturing at me, "have to come and live with me now."

"Mataji, we'll talk about it later. Now you must be tired. Finish your sherry."

Later, in bed, I asked him, "Are you thinking about going back to India?"

"Of course I am. Don't you?"

"I am happy here," I said gently.

"You can be happy there, too. Lots of people are."

"Lots of people are unhappy, too."

"They are only unhappy if they have no money. We have worked hard for ten years now—maybe it is a good time to go back."

"What will you do back there?"

"I will start my own company."

"You could do that here."

"Not the same thing."

"You want to show your old friends, that's all." My throat constricted. I was afraid I would cry.

"So what is wrong with that?"

"It seems . . . it seems so silly. Just when we've begun doing better. I have friends here, people who listen and talk to me, and you have friends too. We just bought this house and Sheila and Nikhil would never get such attention in school in India and . . . and how will you pay your brothers for their share of the house?"

"Don't be stupid, now. You think I want my daughter to paint her face and have a boyfriend by the time she's twelve and my son to join a gang and bring home some New Age junkie? You just leave these decisions to me."

I rolled over with my back to him. I have learned that when anyone wants to control me, they begin by telling me I am stupid.

*

I have a degree from Boston University and I know I am not stupid. Of course, being single while I was there and fearful of damaging my reputation at home, I stayed close to the Indian students and didn't mix with many Americans—that was how I met Prem—but I read and read and learned how to write my résumé and get a job. Being Prem's secretary these few years, I know something about bookkeeping, so I decided I needed to get a job.

Mataji and I were circling one another like two wrestlers in a ring of invisible spectators, demurely passing one another on the stairway and saying "Pehleh aap, pehleh aap" before each doorway. The politeness was excruciating. We feinted gracefully. She noticed I had placed a statue of Saraswati in Sheila's room and lifted the huge brass piece on her tiny shoulders, saying, "What a silly thing, putting a Saraswati statue in a girl's room. Put this goddess where she will do some good, in the boy's room. She's the one who will inspire him to learn." I said nothing, but the next day I moved Saraswati back to Sheila's room. I refuse to apologize for wanting my daughter to be educated.

With the tax season beginning, the temporary agency found me an office job in just a few days. I wore pants to the interview rather than a skirt—I've never learned to walk in a skirt anyway—just so Mataji wouldn't suspect anything. And I said nothing to Prem until I got the call from the agency saying I had been accepted. Then I felt weak with daring.

That night I let Mataji do the cooking and we struggled through the burned results with many "vah-vah, bhai vah" exclamations of wonder. Then I said to Prem, firmly and evenly, "I found a job at an accounting office. I have decided to take it. I start next week."

Prem looked at me as if I had hit him.

"Is this how you repay me?" he said finally.

I was silent. Mataji's delight reared its head and oozed around us like a cobra.

"What have I ever denied you?" he asked. He's using lines from old Hindi movies, I thought. And to think I married him because he was an enlightened, educated Indian.

"Nothing," I said out loud. And in my most reasonable voice, the one I use to explain to Nikhil to be gentle with his little sister, I said, "I have just decided I need to get out during the day and allow Mataji to enjoy the children. That's all."

"*You* have decided! Well," he said, throwing down his napkin. "I hope you enjoy being at someone's beck and call all day. How much is this place going to pay you?"

"Eight dollars an hour."

Mataji said, "Beti, he is only thinking of you—going out to work with all those strange men." She placed another burned chapatti before

Prem.

"Many women work there," I said faintly. I was losing courage.

But then Prem said, "Well, maybe it will help us to save more money so that we can go back to India sooner." Mataji beamed and I thought furiously, Why don't you tell her I don't want us to go back to India. Why don't you say no now instead of raising her hopes? But I had won this round and I knew when to be quiet.

*

It was my mother who saved me from disgrace once by teaching me silence. When Mataji gave away a gold necklace that had been my mother's to some cousin whose dowry she was trying to collect, I was so angry that I went home and told her I was never going back. But my mother wiped my tears and said, "Yes, you are going back. And you are going to be silent. No one will ever be able to say that you were raised to be troublesome. Do you want them to say that all your education only made you like some American feminist?"

"How can you say that if you care for me?" I sobbed.

"I say it because I care for you, little one," said my mother. "Here, is it a gold necklace you want? I'll give you another. But you will have to live with the family who has you now."

"I don't want a gold necklace, I want them to be fair. And what is so wrong to be a feminist?"

My mother thought for a while. Then she said, "Be careful when you use that word. Men become afraid. If you want to survive, you must always let a man believe he has you under control. Silence is an excellent instrument, beti. Use it well."

Then she called my old ayah and told her to escort me back to Mataji's home.

*

But there are limits to silence. I have never liked to discuss money and I began wondering when I would receive my first pay cheque. After four weeks of nothing in the mail, I called the temporary agency and they said, "Oh, didn't you know? Your husband called and told us the account number to which we should send the money, so we've been doing a direct deposit every two weeks."

"Thank you," I said.

That night I asked Prem, when we were in our bedroom and I could hear Mataji's snore droning like a tambura next door, "Why did you call the agency and tell them to send my paycheque to some bank account?"

"Just for convenience." He seemed quite innocent.

"Please would you let me decide what is convenient for me and not convenient for me." My voice was terse, so he started to tease me as if we were back in college.

"Goodness me, she's getting annoyed."

"Yes, I am annoyed. I would have like to see a cheque with my name on it."

"Your name on it? Hardly matters, such a small amount."

"What did you do with it?"

"I put it in the savings account."

"Which one?"

"The one for our return to India."

"I thought so." I sat up in bed. "I told you, I don't want to go back to India. Why do you not just tell Mataji that?"

"Because I want to go back."

The snoring had stopped. I felt the room begin to close in on me, and Prem's face became strange and threatening. I tried a deep breath but the air stopped short in my throat. Something else was straining outward as if to rend the seams that held my mask-face in its place, that same mask-face with which I assured friends on visits to India, "No, of course I have not changed," as if change were some terrible catastrophe that had been so far deftly averted. And then the words took form, delicate bubbles blown in the face of a primordial wind.

"Well, then, go back to India alone."

A different silence fell, as if all our years together were but a sleepy musical alaap to this juncture. If our marriage were a raag, this moment would signal tablas to enter the fray to follow the rise and fall of our heartbeats moving in opposite directions. My mother's voice struck up in my head imploring caution, quiet, restraint.

With Prem's gaze piercing my shoulder blades, I put on my slippers and my housecoat—dressing gown, I mean—and went downstairs to the living room.

Mataji's curiosity emanated from her room as I passed, and she soon joined me on the cushions in front of the fireplace. We stared at the expressionless faces of Ganesh and Shiva together, and finally she couldn't stand it anymore. She said, "What happened? Did you hear a cat crying?"

I picked up her little tape recorder, popped in the right cassette, pressed a button and said, "Yes, Mataji. I was the cat who cried."

The thousand names of Vishnu filled the air.

How I Came to Be a Mexican Indian

MAYA KHANKHOJE

It all started with the Indian Mutiny of 1857, when Indian sepoys serving in the East India company were given new Enfield rifles. To load them, you had to bite on cartridges greased with fat from pigs or cows, and since pigs are regarded as unclean by Moslems and cows as sacred by Hindus, soldiers from either faith were enraged and an uprising ensued. According to official history books, the mutiny was not a popular uprising, a line I had been fed as a schoolchild but which my father quickly made me spit out with a heavy dose of facts.

My father's grandfather, a landed Brahmin, was one of many Indians who participated in this incipient independence movement, which backfired like an Enfield rifle, because the East India Company was stripped of its powers and the British Government settled down in India good and proper. This act of rebellion cost my great grandfather his lands, which in an ironical twist of fate later became the headquarters for Gandhi's nonviolent movement.

Pandurang Sadashiv Khankhoje, my father, was born in Wardha in 1884. His first revolutionary act was to organize a schoolboy boycott of Queen Victoria's Jubilee celebrations by exhorting his classmates not to eat the sweetmeats they were given and to carry out what many years later would be called a "shit and split" on US campuses. His revolutionary activities escalated and the British sentenced him to death in absentia. They were not able to execute him, but they did drive a bullet through his leg, which he carried for the rest of his days. His revolutionary struggles took him all over the world until he finally reached San Francisco, where he worked as a lumberjack while studying military techniques and agriculture. There he and other revolutionaries founded the Gadhar Party.

At some point the American government pulled the welcome mat from under their feet and my father went to Mexico, because he admired the Mexican revolution and wanted to help Mexican peasants. They made him one of their own. The Chinese Nationalist leader Sun Yat Sen had told my father that feeding people was as noble an endeavour as freeing them. Which is why my father became a Mexican citizen in 1929 and decided to play an active role in President Cárdenas's agrarian reform.

My father was then forty-five years old and unmarried, thanks to his vow never to marry unless India became independent. He was to break his vow, as prophesied by a Gypsy fortune-teller who had told him years before that he would marry a blonde woman.

Jeanne Alexandrine Sindic, my mother, a green-eyed blonde beauty, was born in Brussels in 1913, "not far from the Mannequin Piss." Her father, born on the French side, was a freemason who sold sewing machines for a living, and her mother, born on the Flemish side, was a home maker. Her brother had been an antiquarian forced by the postwar economy to become a taxi driver, which was neat, because he drove us all over Brussels when we visited him in 1949.

My parents met in Europe thanks to a thief in the Madrid subway who stole my father's money and papers and forced him to seek help in the Mexican Consulate. There he met Aunt Julia's husband, a Mexican diplomat who befriended him and invited him to dinner.

According to the story, my father was walking up the steps of Aunt Julia's house and my mother was walking down when they ran into each other and a premonitory thought crossed my mother's mind: "I wonder what it would be like to be married to a *black* man?" Years later they met again in Mexico and got married.

My full name is Maya Jeanne Khankhoje y Sindic, Jeanne after my mother and Maya because it is a Mexican as well as an Indian name, and Sindic because Spanish-speaking countries recognize that a mother has something to do with the birth of a child. My sister, Ana Savitri, now a doctor, was born in Guadalajara in 1938, and I was born in

Mexico City in 1942.

After India's independence, my father was invited to head an agricultural commission, so the whole family spent a couple of years in Nagpur, the happiest and most magical in my whole life. Perhaps not quite the happiest, as a deeper kind of happiness would visit me years later with the birth of my two daughters, but certainly magical. Flying to India in 1949 on prop planes was an adventure in itself. It took us one whole week, including a stopover in Gander, where I touched snow for the first time, which stuck to my hand and made it bleed. After twenty years in Canada I now know better!

Those two years in India meant fascinating journeys all over the country, encounters with tigers while sleeping *al fresco*, snakes hiding in the grass, skirmishes with black-faced monkeys, dreamy sessions by the lotus pond, morbid fascination with the dead bodies in the Ganges, tea parties at the Governor's mansion and Hindi lessons from the driver's son, who also taught me how to spit-and-polish shoes.

I wept when we returned to Mexico in 1951 and I wept when we returned to India in 1956, this time for good. A country like India was fascinating to a sever-year-old, but it became constraining to a young girl. But I adapted, rode my bike to school, then to college, where I got a degree in English literature, all the while dreaming of becoming a journalist.

As a university student, I was expected to join the national cadet corps, and as a Mexican citizen, I had to get a special dispensation to serve in the army. There I met my future brother-in-law, who was briefly my commanding officer. The highlight of my part-time military career was to march in the Republic Day parade in Delhi. I was very good at marching but got out of step because the elephants behind me and the camels in front of me distracted me. By the way, marching camels align their necks, not their feet.

On my twentieth birthday, fate took me back to Delhi where I worked as a secretary in the embassies of Venezuela, Bolivia, Uruguay and Peru. I also started free-lancing as a simultaneous interpreter. During one of my interpretation assignments I met the future Secretary of Education of Mexico who offered me a scholarship to study Indian history in Mexico so off I went back to Mexico in 1965.

That year was very eventful. I took up my scholarship, dropped it, met an American student, married him, got pregnant and started my career as a conference interpreter, all in the same year. Nalini Jeanne-Marie was born in 1966 and Shanti Kumari in 1968. They both live in Chicago now. Shanti is a dancer and interpreter and Nalini has worked for the government and for community groups. There was also Do, who took a good look at the harsh world he was born into and decided to return to the void. I never got to touch him, except for the feel of his little body on my stomach while the doctor severed the umbilical cord before he was rushed off to the incubator. He now lies in Las Cruces, overlooking Acapulco Bay.

A word about their father. His name is Charles Johnson González-Casanova and his bloodline also cuts across many borders. His mother had Mayan and Spanish blood but fate took her to be born in New Orleans, instead of in Mexico like her siblings. His father was born in the Midwest but his ancestors were Norwegian. So my daughters have Mayan, Spanish, Norwegian, Indian, Flemish and French blood. So what does that make us, they used to ask. That makes you very pretty, I used to answer. They now know they belong to the human race.

Charles and I are no longer together. The first ten years or so of our marriage were the happiest years of my life, happy not as in magical India, not as in sophisticated New Delhi, not as in exotic travels, not as in creative writer, but happy certainly as in a woman fulfilled. I loved being the companion of an intelligent and loving man and the mother of two lovely girls and a good interpreter and a worthy citizen. I had it all. I had balance and the little black holes of despair that sometimes popped up in my marriage were overwhelmed by the rest.

In 1975 everything started falling apart. That was the year in which my husband had his salary illegally frozen for a year, our house was broken into, our car was stolen, my health was precarious and I had to keep working to feed the family. Then I lost my baby and four days later my husband won his case against the university. Something cracked.

1977 was a sabbatical year. I suggested we go to India to be with my family or France to practise our French. My husband wanted simply to hole up in a small American town with a big library and write a book. As a compromise solution, he opened an atlas and announced that Montreal was the second largest French-speaking city in the world. So we packed our belongings, stuffed them into our bug and drove all the way to Montreal. We stayed there over labour-day weekend just long enough to have a spat. OK you win, I said, so we drove back to the States and rented an empty house close to the Yale University library.

I have little recollection of those nine months, except that I discovered Miller beer and Humphrey Bogart movies. Towards the end I started free-lancing at the United Nations and received a job offer from them and from the International Civil Aviation Organization in Montreal. I chose Montreal with my husband's agreement, so we returned to Montreal in 1978 exactly twenty years ago as I write these pages.

The rest is history, as they say. My husband left me in 1980, returned to Mexico, and now lives in New Orleans. My daughters lived with me, then with him, then with me and now they are on their own. So I have been living "alone" for the last eighteen years, which means there is no man sharing my hearth and home, although there have been men who have touched my heart. And others who have just touched me and gone off on their merry way. And one who touched my heart well before he touched me, but destiny has us living on different continents, and meeting fleetingly by the Seine, or the Rhine, or the St Lawrence or the Danube or the Potomac, and if we cannot meet it doesn't matter, because his voice over the phone still turns my legs to jelly, after all these years and the grandchildren he has acquired in the meantime. And there is another man who touched my soul, but his other life pulled him back so he stopped communicating. But I keep talking to him, because he still inhabits my head.

I live in Montreal and work in a UN Agency and interpret other people's thoughts from one language into another and write my own on paper and dabble in languages and meet with friends and listen to classical music and admire the view from my window. And I travel a lot. China, Egypt, India, Morocco, Western Europe, Eastern Europe, the former Soviet Union, the Amazon Basin, the Galapagos, the breadth and depth of the American continent, and many islands including Cuba and a hug and kiss from the old man.

Or I used to travel. A fragile vessel in my brain has recently clipped my wings somewhat but not broken my spirit. I have now embarked on the most exciting journey of all, a journey of self-discovery into the deep recesses of the mind and beyond. A journey into what the Tibetans call the realm of living and dying.

Wake Up

SHANI MOOTOO

"Angenie. Angenie. Wake up."

My mother softly, urgently calls. Her hand barely touches my shoulder before she pulls it back to herself. She doesn't have to try to wake me. I skip through the night alighting on sleep the way a butterfly barely samples petals of flowers along its path. Even though I am now fourteen I share a room with my two younger sisters, and I'm aware of every change in their breathing patterns as they sleep in their bed. Before my mother walked in I heard her coming, and in a flash I was coherent and in control.

A streetlight has lit a path through the window, across the floor and up one wall. She partially stands in its way, her face alone illuminated. It shows skin swollen with worry and loneliness, her emotions too emaciated to feel anger.

I know this pattern well, having been awakened more times than there are stars in the sky at this blackest hour of the night. Always for comfort and companionship. It would be easier if she asked for money. I could just turn my fat pink plastic pig upside down, rip off its stopper, and willingly shake it empty into her hands. But every time she comes for comforting I feel poor, and desperate to know how best to give her what she steals into my belly for. Instead I stiffen myself into emotionless calm, and take charge, duty of the night nurse.

"Where is your father, Angenie?"

She whispers, cigarette breath suspended over my face. She has been awake long enough for worry to percolate and cause her to smoke. It calms her, to smoke. Or perhaps it is her quiet act of retaliation. If she were to find no solace, soon enough she would resort to Scotch on-the-rocks. The first time we saw her smoke, in the dead of night, as she sat up waiting, we played parent and scolded her to a suspiciously over-belligerent response: she was a grown woman and could do whatever she pleased.

When we first smelled alcohol on her, not the razor-sharp, sweet, racy smell of alcohol that conjures up images of revelry, but an odour made pungent and ominous because of mixing stale breath with sleeplessness and worry, I implored her not to resort to such destructive, degrading means, and Siri and Tara cried. My brother Anil's young face hardened, not toward her, but toward the unacknowledged foe, and he withdrew. After that time she would not awaken the younger ones, and would not allow me to see her smoke and drink. Never more than one cigarette or drink, mind you, and slowly, painstakingly, consumed. But her bathroom, with the blue cooped-up haze, its unmistakable smell, and her breath, won't hide themselves. Her own rebellion. Asserting that, at least in her own eyes, she can maintain some modicum of power on these crazy nights when she feels less than a wife.

I cannot bear to tell her that I don't know where he is. Not that she actually expects that I would know, but I wish I could hold up a candle for her.

Not to wake up Siri and Tara, I ask back in a sliver of voice, "Daddy has not come home as yet?"

She shakes her head and purses her lips.

"What time is it?"

"It's three-fifteen. Come."

Come. Come into her bedroom. To sit and offer wisdom, companionship, solace. Subordination and authority given to me to juggle in the same hand like double-edged swords. Come. A strange demand at a time like this. It is not a request where the response might be a flower bud unfolding of itself to offer and give deliverance, but rather a command, a hand reaching into one's intestines and ripping out yard after yard, desperately searching for things it has not even defined.

Yet I get up efficiently, as if this were the time one naturally arose from bed, acutely aware that I am the chosen one in this hour of a grown-up's chaos. I hold my breath so as not to make a sound that would bring my sisters, or Anil, in his room across from ours, out of sleep, and jeopardize the coveted one to oneness I find myself afforded with my mother on those nights.

It is a cold night made suddenly colder. Already my neck muscles have become stiffer. My exterior, however, does not appear shaken. My mother needs me to calm her, not encourage her fears with my own.

A little girl with a frightened mother who might just as well be blind are the only passengers in a rowboat that has a leak, tossing and tumbling about in the midst of a grey-and-silver vicious storm, clods of rapid-fire rain slashing into their eyes, the most awful crashing, cracking of the sky, and the little girl quickly deciphering the shadows of monsters lurking hungrily in the waves across the shoreless expanse of Atlantic seas. She calms and comforts and reassures her mother; she bales out water gushing up from the leak and from the waves crashing over the tiny boat; she takes off her shirt and wraps it around her mother's shoulders; she materializes a fire out of thin air to warm her poor frightened mother, and rows the boat to eventual safety, all the while taking pains to cajole the sinking morale of her mother in a voice controlled, calm and gentle.

"Where is your father? What could he be doing at this hour? I can't go on like this any longer, I do everything for you all, I've devoted my life to you all, I have never neglected my responsibilities, I've been a damn good wife, and this is what I get in return. I should have been a wife like all those other women, their husbands don't even know where they are in the middle of the day, your father does not know how lucky he is, I can't go on like this, what should I do? I only stay with your father because of you all, you know, not a damn thing has changed in these fifteen years since we got married. You're the eldest, Angenie, if only you were a boy, but I have to call on you, I am so lonely, I don't want to spend the rest of my life worrying where your father is, what am I going to do, look at my hands, they're shaking, look at my face, I am a wreck, I can't go on living like this, I just wish I could die."

I sit in the chair beside the bed, physically distanced. She sits propped against pillows in her bed, her toes curled back hard and her hands wrapping and unwrapping and wringing and unwringing a handkerchief.

She begins crying, a low wailing cry. More like a sound coming through her than from her. As if she were giving voice to all her female ancestors and they were all wailing at the same moment.

How inadequate I feel around her. Had I been, as the first offspring, a boy, I could have taken the situation more effectively in hand and offered her a strong, firm shoulder. I want to reach over and touch her, but there is no invitation. To do so would be inappropriate, not the stuff that our relationship is made of. I imagine how I would touch her if I did get the go-ahead, but to do so I must frame my protection of her in television images of the cowboy heroes I so envy.

A cowboy moves to the edge of her bed. He sits next to her on her left. He puts his right arm around her shoulders and gently draws her against him. He is a warm wall to lean into, a tall silent man, with long hard limbs, and men fear him. He speaks no words, but she feels safe and is calmed. She knows that he will not take advantage of her. In his gentleness she feels his outrage at her hurt. He wants revenge for her.

"Mummy, don't do that to yourself. He's probably gone for a drink with the people from the meeting."

"At three-thirty? Those people have all gone home already. Whose husband is going to go drinking at this hour? Those people all have jobs that they have to get up and go to. Your father is not out at any bar. He is out with some woman."

The other times, he never even tried to hide the lipstick on the collar of his crisp white shirts or on his white handkerchiefs. She could be right this time. It almost makes one succumb to belief in the supernatural, the way she always know where he is or what he is doing. As if she has penetrated his subconcious. Years of being burnt has taught her to infiltrate his brain and lodge herself somewhere in his psyche where she can read his every twitch and thought. She has never, however, learned to redirect him, reprogram him from the little niche she lives in inside his brain. Of what use, then, this infiltration? She at least is able to guess where he is, and so has some hook to hang on to when she can't find him on the telephone. As much as her imaginings make her fraught with anguish, having no idea whatever about where he is would be worse. Perhaps it affords her the illusion of being in control. Of not being totally in the dark.

But tonight I would prefer if she were wrong. Even if that meant that he might came home slovenly and obnoxiously drunk. I could almost welcome him beating pots and pans at this ungodly hour when on past occasions he has insisted, with a drunk man's determination, on cooking a curry with frozen beef, for forty people. A project he would abandon halfway as alcohol-induced sleep took over. I would gratefully sleep through that commotion tonight, relieved.

But being with another woman! It was a small jump from imagining him rejecting his wife to imagining him rejecting his children. Rejecting his family. Utter chaos. Utter shame. A shame he has taught us to have. Never forget that all men are bastards, he says, and I wonder if he partly intends to include himself in the pronouncement of this simple truth, and so to excuse himself from being one. But I, family, automatically exempt him from this.

A flash of loathing rises up in me and instantly subsides as it meets a wall that wills him to be out drinking.

"Mummy, you're letting your imagination run away with you. I can understand why you think he is with someone else, but I am sure, as sure as you are about where he is, that he is only out having a few drinks. He is probably not doing anything wrong. He just has a lot of worries and needs to go out and forget them for a while. He works so hard and then he goes to meetings. He never has time for relaxing. And if he comes home we all want help with homework. People are always phoning, are always coming. He needs a little time of his own. You're worrying yourself for nothing."

Her face has changed. She seems reassured, and leans back a little more relaxed. And I find myself praying to the stars that I am right. If I am right we will remain a family intact. If I am right she will call on me again. How easily she believes anything that makes her feel better.

Almost four in the morning. I have to get up for school in two hours.

Suddenly she is out of bed and lunging at the bathroom light to turn it off. Nervously she hurries back into bed.

"Listen! He is here. Go on back to bed quickly."

I still cannot hear the car so I hesitate, listening. I hear nothing.

"What are you waiting for? I said go to bed. Do you want him to come in and catch us awake? You know how badly he will behave if he is drunk. Go to bed.''

Catch us. As if we were the ones at fault. Once he came home hours after midnight and found us waiting up, worried, and he behaved as if that act were itself an accusation.

And now I hear the low hum at the gate. How well her ears know the sound of his car from so far away. From all the nights she has sat alone in the dark and picked it out above the rustling of the coconut trees, and amongst the other cars on the highway.

In a voice sharpened with fear she snaps, ''Go!'' And I know that my position is subordinate again. I go.

In the darkness I see that Siri's eyes are open. Light from the corridor bounces off the whites of her eyes in little beams. We do not speak to each other. I wonder if Tara, in the same bed, and Anil in his room, are also awake in their dark corners, aware of everything. I feel a flicker of disgust that they did not come to our mother's rescue when she most wanted it. And then arrogant pride that I am the one who could be counted on in an emergency.

I slip into bed noiselessly, and hold my breath. I cover my face with my arm so that my shut eyes would not be seen flickering in fright in case my father were to look in on us.

His footsteps are sure, not those of a drinking man. Perhaps the meeting was indeed a very long one. Faint sounds of hushed, clipped talking come from my parents' room. Relieved at the thought of quiet in the remaining hours of dark, I relax, and drift quickly toward sleep.

A coconut estate. Near a fence. Three of us lie on the uncovered ground of crabgrass and dried coconut branches. In a window of a house outside the fence, the upper body of a man paces back and forth. He is unaware of us, but I am anxious that he might look over and see us. The girl lying on my right talks incessantly. I do not know what she is saying. On my left is a person, older, female. My body gathers heat from hers. I wish the girl on my right would leave us alone. I wish so hard that she disappears. Now we are alone. The fingers of my left hand fall open and touch the woman's skirt. I want to hold her. I want her to hold me. My heart beats a ferocious tune.

The man in the window paces, unaware. I roll onto one elbow and move my face towards hers. Slowly my mouth is lowered onto hers. Her lips press back onto mine, but only so briefly that I am left standing outside of myself looking at us, wishing to know more. And then, suddenly, she has turned away. My own desires insist on being heard but no amount of begging and tugging will bring her back. I am afraid that she might even be dead. Her face becomes recognizable; it is my mother's, and seeing this, I demand with the power of an impetuous, desperate kiss that she not desert me.

Siri and Tara are up and almost dressed for school when I open my eyes. My heart is racing and I can feel the muscles of my face contorted by the passion and pain of a kiss, a kiss that is fast evaporating. Colours and details of my dream have begun to fade but my chest holds tangled, knotted vestiges of grief, and pleasure, of moments of invincibility, and terror; confusions that could be assuaged by that kiss.

Bring back the kiss . . .

Until I remember that the face of the woman was my mother's.

How could I possibly have dreamt this! Perhaps I was mistaken; it was not my mother whom I kissed. But I recall the dream, and hard as I try I cannot replace her face with someone else's. The chaos in my chest abruptly gels to expose a singular shame. Worst of all is that such a dream would come out of me mere hours after I was privy to her brittleness.

I cover my face with the blanket and wonder what kind of a monster I am. How can I face her? She is bound to know when she sees me.

"Angenie. Do you realize what time it is? It's ten to seven. You're going to be late for school. Get up!"

My mother stands over me. The skin of her face is puffy, awake-all-night skin. Her tired, heavy eyes, and mouth taut at the ends contain a crying fighting rage. She looks like a rope stretched so tightly that it is about to snap. She is not aware of my dream. Commanding me to get up for school, she attempts to sever any bond from last night.

Looking at her face I try to see in it a person with whom I could have enjoyed even the less odious act of hugging. I am pleased that I have not the remotest desire for her. Repulsion (the less damning edge of guilt) for kissing my mother, even if it was only in a dream, follows me around as I get up and prepare for school. Where do dreams come from? What inside of me could have created such a dream?

"Where was Daddy last night?" I ask, forcing her to acknowledge that she had broken down in front of me only hours ago. Yet I know full well that she will give only enough of an answer to justify her angst, and brush away admission of my father's slight toward her. Now, in the light of day, her bravery does not need propping, and she will not tolerate any hint of criticism of him.

"He says the meeting was late."

"Do you believe him?"

She bites the corner of her lower lip and curtly replies, "No."

I don't want to overstep my boundaries by asking where she thinks he was. What I feel for her this morning is decidedly not desire, not even the desire of a cowboy to protect her, but disgust. Last night when she opened her wounds for me to see, and when she asked me to wait up with her, I would have climbed mountains to deliver her. But this morning, as she denies me, I despise her for spinelessness. For cringing in the face of my father's philandering. I despise her role of excellent wife who stands behind the successful husband, of mother of polite well behaved and smart schoolchildren. I despise her for staying, for the way she allows herself to be hurt, the way she accepts it.

The woman before me and the woman I kissed in my dream have the same features but my feelings toward them are vastly different.

Being female, my future looks grim, claustrophobic. I worry that I am expected, as a girl, to grow up to be just like her. The alternative to being just like her is to be just like him. And as much as I cry inside at his rejection of her and so of us, his freedom looks more exciting, interesting. The freedom to work, to go to meetings, to speak his mind; the freedom to go out with the "boys" until way into the early morning hours, to smoke, to drink, to have adventures. The freedom, inherent in his maleness, to philander. What he does with the freedom is another matter. Still, the fantasy of modelling myself in his image (with modifications to the details, mind you) is more honourable than consenting to spending a lifetime trapped by the body of a female.

If I were afforded such independence I would see the world, ride a bicycle from Alaska to Tiera Del Fuego, hike in Bhutan, snorkel above the Great Barrier Reef, befriend Prince Charles, wrestle with him at polo, and then later that day talk with him about great world archietecture. I would make paintings like the one of Dorian Gray. I would write Somerset Maugham. I would disguise myself as a boy and one would never know that I was a girl.

Besides obvious fear, the mere thought of Mummy fills me with sadness. I no longer expect to be able to please her, and passively accept this. But, even though it seems impossible to do, I have an unquenchable thirst for pleasing Daddy. His boldness and bravery are intimidating. I am afraid of him and admire him. I am cautious to loathe his actions, not him.

I have not seen him this morning as yet. I am avoiding him. It is time to leave for school and I must say goodbye to them both.

But I can hardly look him in his eyes. Perhaps I'd rather not see evidence of his rejection of us, of another woman in his smile or his voice. What did he do with her last night? Did he kiss her? Did my father touch her breasts? Did he lie down with her? Did she hold his face in her hands, did her do to her what he does with Mummy? There is no enjoyment in this!

I hardly hear what is being taught at school today. For one thing, I am unbearably tired. For another, I have pictures in my head of my mother lying in bed crying; of my father making love to a plethora of strange women; of a jealous woman poisoning her husband; of a raging madwoman stabbing herself and her children; of a cowboy bringing his wagon and putting the woman and her children in it and riding off with them to a sprawling homestead in the country, far away from other people.

Porous Borders

ROSHNI RUSTOMJI

My mother left me three legacies worth talking about. A black shawl she had been embroidering for me as a PhD graduation present. A long-haired, blonde wig she bought herself when the wretched chemicals that were to cure her killed her hair. And she left me her friendship with Ushabehen.

We never did know Ushabehen's real family name. She used different last names at different times. We knew her as Ushabehen Mehta, Ushabehen Sethi, Ushabehen Mazumdar. At one time she announced that she was Ushabehen Ramirez and at another time that she was Ushabehen King. My younger sister Shireen and I used to call her Ushabehen Soap Warrior because of the way we met her.

It was on a Friday afternoon in June. I was thirteen years old and Shireen was about to turn eleven. She was engaged as usual in some perspiration-encouraging activity such as bicycling round and round the block or just running through every neighbour's backyard, screaming at the top of her voice. I think it was the latter because every now and then I heard Mrs Murphy, our neighbour to the left of us, shouting, "Shireen, stop screaming like a banshee! It is time you learned to act like a lady!" Of course it wasn't very ladylike of Mrs Murphy to be yelling, but then Shireen did inspire people to break their usual behaviour patterns. I was working on a jigsaw puzzle titled "The Great Prairie" on the kitchen table. Just as I was about to finish the wide-open blue sky, my mother walked into the room and announced that it was time for her to take us for our annual checkup at Dr Simon's office.

Three minutes after the nurse had taken Shireen into the examination room, we heard her wailing, "Mamma! Mamma!" Mother ran to the room and I followed her.

Shireen was sitting straight up on the examination cot and crying, "She's horrible! I am not—Mamma, I am not—" She was also trying to attack the nurse with her fists and her feet. Shireen was good at such things. I usually ran away from her whenever she began to fight. Dr Simon had also rushed into the room and amidst Shireen's cries and continuing attempts at kicking and hitting the nurse, we discovered that Shireen was unhappy and enraged because the nurse had said, "You awful child, you stink." Dr Simon knew us well. He said, "No, no Miss Johnson. It's just honest sweat. Shireen likes to play games and climb trees." "No, it's not that," said Nurse Johnson. "This child has that peculiar smell. These people always have this awful smell. They are dirty. Damn them."

A woman in a pink polyester pantsuit and a bindi on her forehead wandered into the examination room just in time to hear Nurse Johnson's pronouncement. A strong smell of jasmines entered the room with her. The woman rushed to the sink in the corner of the room, grabbed the antiseptic soap from the sink, ran water over the soap, went to Nurse Johnson and began to rub the wet soap across her mouth. "Bad words. Bad words. Wrong. Wrong!" said the woman. Nurse Johnson tried to get away, yelling, "Get out! Your appointment is not till half an hour from now. How dare you come into this room!" My mother moved in between Nurse Johnson and the woman and quietly took the soap away. The woman then turned to Dr Simon and said: "This is what my son Ramesh's teacher told me to do to him when he uses bad language. She told me to wash out his mouth with soap."

And that is how we met Ushabehen, and that is when Ushabehen became my mother's dearest friend.

We knew nothing about Ushabehen's past history in India and very little about what had happened to her in America before we met her. And I cannot tell you what she looked like. But I can tell you about the sound and the smell of her.

The smell of jasmines was Ushabehen's olfactory shadow. Sometimes it was a soft perfume. Just a gentle smell of early mornings and babies right after their baths. And sometimes it was an overwhelming, stick-to-your-nose, sweet smell. The odour of life gone wrong, things in decay.

And no one could ever forget Ushabehen's voice. It was loud, deep and raw. Ushabehen usually turned her complaints and anger into laughter. Laughter that often made us uneasy. And even as children, Shireen and I heard fragments of pain and wounded bewilderment in Ushabehen's voice. Shireen once said to me, "Rhoda, something awful must have happened to Ushabehen. Her voice sometimes sounds like freshly grated coconut. Nice and tasty but all shredded up."

When we were young, Shireen and I were prone to embarrassment regarding our Indian-accented elders. But we were never embarrassed by Ushabehen. Not even when she hummed, or muttered, or sang loudly and defiantly the one line of the one song she knew, "Jaraa hatke, jaraa fatke yeh he Mumbai meri jaan." We weren't embarrassed even when she rendered the Hindi into her English version of "With a moving here and a pushing there, *this*, my dear, is *Bombay*!" She sang the line constantly. In her home, in our home, at the pharmacy where she worked, in restaurants, in shops, while waiting for buses and even while walking down our usually sedate street in Dallas. In order to make our mother laugh, Ushabehen would sometimes vary the line. She would drop Mumbai and would sing, "Yeh he Dallas" or "Yeh he Texas" or "Yeh he Remember the Aalaamo-faalaamo" or "Yeh he Mickey Mouse" or "Yeh he very good sized prawns" or "Yeh he complete madness-fadness-my-dear."

It was again a Friday afternoon in June, twelve years after the soap incident, when we were informed that Shireen had died in Vietnam. Ushabehen came to be with my mother for forty days and forty nights. Her voice and the smell of jasmines comforted us. She agreed with my mother that since Shireen's body was not found, Shireen was not dead. She was just wounded and lost. Somewhere in Asia. The two women refused to mourn. They were holding a vigil to help my sister find her way back home. And yes, Ushabehen did sing about our Shireen and in the present tense, "Yeh he hamari Shireen, meri jaan," as she helped my mother around the house. And my mother sang along with her.

My sister and Ushabehen's son, Ramesh, had been sent off to Vietnam within a month of each other. Shireen was an army nurse. Ramesh was in the Air Force. Both had selected their professions right after high school to prove they were the best Americans from India that one could ever be.

Eight months after Shireen's death, Ramesh's body was mailed back to the United States in the requisite box, covered with the requisite flag. My mother went to stay with Ushabehen for forty days and forty nights.

In his last letter to Ushabehen, Ramesh had informed her that he had fathered a son in Vietnam and that he was planning to bring him to America at the end of the war.

On the forty-first day after Ramesh's body arrived in the United States, Ushabehen said to my mother, "You need to go and bring Ramesh's son to America."

"Why me? You should go, Ushabehen. I'll help you to go to Vietnam and to bring your grandchild back here."

"Can't," said Ushabehen.

"Why can't you?" asked my mother.

"Because if I leave, I can't come back."

"Why?"

"Because I have no papers. Not to be here and not to be where I came from."

"I'll get you papers. For America." My mother could take things in her stride. And she was resourceful.

"I don't want any papers-fapers. I just want my grandchild. You go. Find my grandchild. Look for Shireen. Bring them both back."

And so my mother went to Southeast Asia and came back with a girl about six years old named Tara.

Ushabehen was somewhat surprised at getting a granddaughter instead of a grandson but my mother's explanation satisfied her.

According to my mother, she was unable to find Ramesh's son in Vietnam. The United States Air Force wouldn't help her. It had more important things on its mind. The war wasn't going well. Which wasn't too surprising since wars usually don't go well. So mother went to Cambodia because she thought she would find Shireen there. She had dreamed of Shireen against the ruins of Angkor Wat. Instead of Shireen, she found a little girl hiding in the forest on the edge of one of the minor ruins. The girl followed mother to the cycle rickshaw my mother had hired, got into the rickshaw and told the man who drove the rickshaw to take her to her grandmother. My mother and the rickshaw driver, who turned out to be a student of Sanskrit and a lover of Indian films, spent three weeks looking for a grandmother who would claim the little girl. When no such grandmother was found by them, the rickshaw driver persuaded my mother that the girl was a reincarnation of Shireen and that she should be taken back to America. When I heard this explanation, I told mother and Ushabehen that although I, as a professor of mathematics, was the only functioning mathematician among the three of us, even a non-mathematician could figure out that the child was born before Shireen died.

No one ever dared to ask my mother how she had been able to take a child out of Cambodia and bring her into the United States. As I said, my mother was a resourceful woman. And she was also as rationally, awe-inspiringly and inflexibly persuasive as Sita, Savitri and Eleanor Roosevelt combined. I suspect she used the Red Cross, various adoption agencies and maybe even Canada to smuggle Tara in. And then she somehow managed to get Tara genuine, legal American citizenship.

My mother died two years after she brought Tara to America. She died still believing that Shireen was alive. Somewhere in Asia.

A few months after my mother died, Tara began to talk about the strange sounds she heard every night and the terrible nightmares that haunted her right into the middle of the day. Sounds and dreams from the first years of her life when she had wandered around looking for her grandmother. Ushabehen tried to dispel them with her love and with teas and herbs and medications and chants and prayers. But the sounds and the nightmares persisted.

When she was about thirteen years old, Tara came to spend a few days with me at my house in Pescadero. It was early January. We went to walk on the beach one evening to see if we could sight at least one migrating whale on the horizon. Tara had announced that morning that she had heard the whales singing all night long as they travelled within a few miles of my house. Across the broccoli-, brussels sprouts- and flower-growing fields, across the freeway continuously threatened by sand dunes, across the marsh, the beach and the rocks, Tara had heard the whales from within the ocean at midnight. We saw no whales, observed no sudden spouts of water in the distance. We ended up watching pelicans dive-bombing the Pacific Ocean for their evening meal.

Tara had just started high school when she chose to deal with her nightmares through the way of drugs. Ushabehen took her to doctors and counsellors and hospitals and half-way houses and treatment centres but no one could help her.

One day, when Tara was still a freshman, Ushabehen phoned me to tell me that she was coming to California.

I picked her up at San Francisco airport and drove us to a restaurant specializing in vegetarian food. The shadow of a slowly circling buzzard appeared and disappeared, again and again, etched dark against the dried grass of the hills next to the restaurant. Ushabehen looked at the menu and said, "Yeh he healthy-felthy restaurant, meri jaan." While our waitress was taking our order, Ushabehen sang softly, "Yeh waitress is a nakh-nu-ticchku, noseee is in the air, meri jaan." And that was true. The waitress was barely polite as she took our order and then the order of the elderly couple sitting a few tables to our left. I was surprised that Ushabehen didn't sing about the couple. They weren't overly polite either. They were staring at us and quite obviously talking about us.

Ushabehen pulled out a map of North America from her bag, pushed aside the dried flower arrangement from the middle of our table and spread the map between us. As she leaned over the map I smelt a trace of the old jasmine perfume.

"Ushabehen, can I please have a bottle of the jasmine perfume you make?" I asked.

"This is no time for perfume talk, Rhodabeh. Tara has disappeared. I have to find her." And Ushabehen started tracing the line of demarcation between the United States and Mexico.

"It goes bumping up and down. Who made it?"

"What?"

"This line. It looks more like holes in a sieve joined together."

"Where is Tara, Ushabehen?"

Ushabehen said, "I want your mother's hair."

I didn't know what she was talking about. So she raised that good, strong voice of hers and repeated her request in Gujarati, "Mane tara Mamma na baal joiyech."

The older couple on our left nearly jumped out of their chairs. The waitress came briskly towards us.

Ushabehen didn't pay attention to anything that was going on. She raised her voice a bit louder, "I want your mother's wig. Her blonde w-e-e-e-g, Rhodabeh, meri jaan."

My mother and Ushabehen were the only people who called me Rhodabeh instead of Rhoda.

By now the waitress had reached us. "Ma'am," she said. "Please lower your voice. You are disturbing the other customers."

Ushabehen raised her voice even louder, "Jaraa hatke, jaraa fatke, this is a very rude waitress, we won't tip her, meri jaan."

At this point the waitress said something that sounded suspiciously like, "Oh shit. A drunk!" She tried to move Ushabehen's chair, with Ushabehen in it. Ushabehen began to laugh and demanded soap to wash out the young woman's mouth. I jumped up to stop the waitress from unseating Ushabehen but the older couple who had been staring at us had already reached her. The woman was trying to get the waitress away from Ushabehen by pulling on her ponytail. The man was helping Ushabehen rise from the chair. The waitress was yelling at the manager to call the police. I was adding to the confusion by demanding our bill. Ushabehen continued to sing about the waitress. The four other customers who were in the restaurant were watching us, trying to decide if they should interfere in what most probably looked like a cross between an interracial sit-com and the *Twilight Zone*. With two brown aliens at the centre of the action. Not always the most comfortable position to find oneself in when members of the SaDiAV gang, the San Diego Airport Vigilantes, roamed at will throughout California and could be checking up on us anytime, anywhere. Even in vegetarian restaurants. Even on a fogless, serene autumn afternoon of buzzards and red-tailed hawks.

As the restaurant manager began to walk towards us, the old gentleman who had persuaded his wife to let go of the waitress's hair, led his wife, Ushabehen and myself out of the restaurant and into the parking lot.

"We heard you talking Gujarati," he said.

"Yes," said the woman. "My husband and I were in India. We followed Gandhiji for a year. He was a great man. We learned a little bit of Hindi and a little bit of Gujarati."

"You followed Gandhiji in India and pulled that poor woman's hair in California!" Ushabehen was laughing.

And then she began to cry. Without any sound. There were no sobs. No trying to catch a breath. There were just tears. After a few seconds, she blew her nose and said, "All I was trying to do is ask Rhodabeh for her mother's wig."

"Of course you can have it. But why?"

"Because Tara is gone. One of her friends came to my house yesterday to tell me that Tara was trying to get away from drugs and she told the police about a man who sold drugs to her friends—just as I told her to do if the man came near her—and the man got very angry and told her he would kill her and me. Tara got very scared and instead of coming to me, she ran away. She told her friend that if she went to Mexico, the man would think she was dead and then he wouldn't hurt me. I have to go to Mexico and I have no papers and I want to disguise myself and go."

"Won't work," said the man, who had introduced himself as John Gregory and his wife as Joy Gregory.

"Yes, it will. I was a Hollywood starlet once upon a time," Joy Gregory said. "Follow us in your car. We live only a few miles from here."

And so we followed them to their house. I remonstrated all the way at this rather unexpected and possibly dangerous course of action. Ushabehen told me to stop worrying.

Joy Gregory showed Ushabehen how to apply makeup. First there were layers upon layers of flesh-toned foundation creams. Creams of different flesh tones that started with what looked like a beige and ended up with a final cover of what looked like a mask made of melted-together tutti-frutti ice cream. A blend, a whirl of milk-chocolate brown, Melanta white and synthetic strawberry-pink. A mask that might possibly fool someone into thinking that Ushabehen was sporting a Southern California tan over what could be a basic pink and white complexion. All this went onto Ushabehen's hands and face. Then there was a bit of lipstick, a bit of rouge, a bit of eye shadow on the face. While Joy was working on her, Ushabehen told her about my mother and Shireen and Ramesh and Tara and she memorized the makeup process. Loudly. Like a child memorizing her multiplication tables. When she was finished with the makeup, Joy pulled out a pair of green nonprescription contact lenses and an auburn wig from a hat box. As she fitted the lenses and the wig onto Ushabehen, she explained that these were from her "Go as Lillith the Witch" Halloween ensemble. And then Joy gave Ushabehen her passport and told her, "From now until you find your granddaughter and bring her back, you are Joy Gregory going on a visit to Mexico. When anyone asks you for your papers, just show this passport. They'll think the woman in the photograph has dyed her hair and gotten new eye colour in an attempt to look younger.

I thought the whole scheme was crazy and offered to go myself to find Tara. But Ushabehen refused. "No. This time I will go."

Before I took her to the airport, Ushabehen looked at herself in the mirror in my hallway and started laughing, "Look Rhodabeh. Jaraa hatke, jaraa fatke yeh he Ushabehen-Joy meri jaan!" And she gave me a bottle of her jasmine perfume.

And she flew over that porous border.

About two weeks later, when I returned from a conference in Boston, I got a phone call from Joy. Ushabehen had been trying to reach me to tell me that she had been arrested in Mexico City but everything was fine now. She had been released and was on her way home.

"With or without Tara?" I asked

"With her granddaughter. The young woman was trying to beg in Mexico City, dressed up as one of those clowns. You know the ones who perform for the motorists who stop at traffic lights."

I said I didn't know. I hadn't been to Mexico and I really didn't think Tara would ever dress up as a clown.

Joy assured me that she knew from her own experience that one would dress up as Kafka's indeterminate insect if one had to. Ushabehen found her granddaughter when a taxi driver told her of a fight between the regular performers-for-pesos and a foreigner. A young girl from China or from India, he said. When Ushabehen approached Tara, Tara tried to run away. In the ensuing chase Ushabehen lost her wig and her makeup started to crack and fall down her face and onto her chest in multicolored flakes. Even then, nothing would have happened if Tara had not fallen down and the police hadn't thought that Ushabehen was trying to kidnap Tara. The police arrested them both. When they discovered that there had been no kidnap attempt and that Ushabehen claimed Tara as her granddaughter, they released the two women.

Ushabehen had told Joy that she would call me as soon as she reached the United States.

She called very late one evening. She said "Rhoda, I am still in Mexico. Don't say anything. Just listen to me. I am calling from one of those public phone places and I don't have too much money left and I have to hurry. Tara and I are going to cross the border. Into California. That drug man followed her to Mexico and thinks we will come into Texas. I have to smuggle us back in. She ran off without any papers and since I lost all my make-up and all that stuff, I really can't use Joy's passport. They will arrest me for stealing her passport. And then they will deport me. Don't worry. After all, it's nothing. Jaraa hatke, jaraa fatke, just a few steps from here to there, meri jaan. I'll be in touch." And then she hung up.

But she did not keep in touch.

About a week and a half after Ushabehen's phone call, I got a call from a police officer. He wanted me to identify two women. They had been shot somewhere near an isolated trailer park in the mountains around San Diego. The mountains that look as if a treacherous lunar landscape had been set on fire and burned brown before being dumped onto North America.

The police officer was vague about what had happened. He spoke about two strange women being seen wandering around the mountains, near the trailer park. There was also a man in the vicinity. The officer didn't know if the man was with the women or if he was following them. He wouldn't tell me much more. Joy and I found out later from some newspaper accounts that when some of the trailer park dwellers sighted the three strangers, obviously trying to use their territory to enter into the United States of America, they decided it was time for action. About fifteen of the trailer park residents, women and men, got into five sturdy vehicles and tracked down the two women. The man eluded them. They pursued the two women with honking of horns and lights on high beams until they were able to pin them against the wall surrounding the trailer park. Someone called 911. The police and the man who had followed Tara from Dallas to Mexico to California arrived at the scene at the same time. There were conflicting reports as to who fired what and how many shots at whom. The two women and the man were killed. The older woman had twelve dollars, an American passport issued to Joy Gregory and a piece of paper with my name and phone number in the pocket of her pants.

Joy and I flew down to San Diego and drove to the morgue. I wish I could say that I smelled jasmines when the two faces were uncovered. I couldn't smell anything. And there wasn't even a memory of songs or whales in the vicinity of the two bodies. When the man asked me, "Ma'am, can you identify these two women?" All I could say was, "No, I can't. How can I? There is such a God awful silence in here." It was left to Joy Gregory to identify Ushabehen and Tara, to make their funeral arrangements and to tell me that it was time for me to go and search for my sister in Asia.

Lekythos

LAKSHMI GILL

Standing on the icy pavement in her brown boots and woolen jacket, she turned to look behind her at the heavy door she had just closed. Through the living-room window she could see her five-and-a-half-year-old son Jason and four-year-old daughter Lyn watching "Disney." Somewhere in the kitchen her husband Don would be stirring his after-supper cup of coffee twenty times in preparation to sitting on his favourite chair to read the *Globe and Mail*. The warm glow of the frosted swag lamp settled in the room.

Outside, the trees were icy shafts against a clear, dark sky. They pierced her as did the cold New Brunswick February night air. She tugged at her jacket and deliberately but with heavy tread walked briskly towards the campus.

She had borrowed the office of a friend, an English professor on sabbatical leave, where she had set up Don's manual typewriter. It would be a worthwhile novel, worth the leaving of her family every six o'clock since December. The night she informed Don about her desire to write away from home, his facial muscles fell. The mouth collapsed into the jowl at her audacity to whip through the washing and drying of dishes, wave goodbye and whiz off. He had continued to object for three months because it was, after all, he who went back to his office every night after supper to catch up on his work. Between the roast and the potatoes, he dropped comments that made her feel inadequate as a mother and a woman, but she closed her heart and eyes to him and persisted. She shut off, as well, the image of her children's faces. At first, taking their cue from Don's loud recriminations, they had clung to her and barred her way out the door. But, perhaps because they saw her again when they woke up in the morning, now they simply waved back without hesitation.

In fifteen minutes she was inside the dimly lit building. She ran up the steps to the third floor. The keys brushing against their ring echoed in the empty hallway. She shuddered. This was a dangerous undertaking. So much safer at home with the family around her. Someone could be waiting in the shadows; someone who knew her routine.

Quickly, she slid into the office. The wheat-coloured walls embraced her. The red drapes were closed just as she had left them. Slowly, she groped her way to the desk lamp. In a second, the light illuminated the circle of typewriter and manuscript.

She sat down and gazed at the magic circle. Writing. Why did she do it? Why did language urge its way through her, transmit itself down to her fingertips? She would spend four hours here, making black marks on a white page. Meanwhile, someone at home could be dying. What were her priorities? Each night she questioned herself as she went over Don's facial contortions and his words that hurt her deeply. These pressed against her; yet each night, here she was, defiantly making spectral marks on her black soul.

Letters leaped at her, begging her to use them. Take me, said an M. Why not an A? D? M A D ? Each letter lay before her in a sensuous pose, beguiling her. The erotics of an alphabet. In the beginning, as a child, it was a game. She had loved words and enjoyed the act of putting them together, to force them into focus and meaning. But now that she was a mother, writing became her jail-keeper, her addiction, her temptation, that which compelled her to leave home to brave the winter night and freeze her fingers in a cold, borrowed office. Her rewards were marital discord and arthritis: punishments for this seduction.

The manuscript stirred. Her dead sister came to life. She sat at the edge of the desk, legs dangling, one shoe caught at a toe. "I'm grateful, Robin, that you're writing this novel about me and Peter for Matthew. He was so young when we died."

"Twenty months," she sighed.

"He never knew us. Now he's seventeen. All those years we lost. Remember how, in San Francisco, I wouldn't even let anyone hold him or carry him when he was a baby? Now all kinds of strangers have held him."

"Sis, this is all worthwhile, isn't it? To give him his parents?"

Her sister glided across the room to the bookshelves. "Books, books. So many written words. What long hours were spent on these. Whole lifetimes."

"As I do this for Matthew, I lose my Jason and Lyn."

"They give up their lives for a work of art." Her sister disappeared into a Dickens.

The light blazed and flickered as Robin saw again their mangled bodies against the poplars and heard again the crunch of Army truck on their tiny car. She took up her pen and wrote as though each word were a jagged piece of metal slicing her flesh, carving up her body for a banquet of the gods. After four hours of continuous writing, her arms and neck ached, her legs were numb.

She locked up the office and walked home feeling the weight of the world on her slight frame. Snowflakes on her coal-black hair and humped shoulders weighted her down even more. The town was quiet, the streets were empty. Only the snow on the trees moved in the wind, fell on the white ground in large clumps.

The children were asleep. Don sat as always in front of the TV, an open book on his lap, beer glass on the floor beside his brown recliner. Since he spoke all day with students and colleagues in the psychology department, he was all talked out by the time he got home. Robin, whose dialogue consisted of "eat your supper," "not again," and other brilliant comebacks longed to discuss news, theories, anything with an adult. But he responded with noncommittal "uh-huhs" so she learned to be quiet, to keep all her quiet deep within her.

She poured herself a Coke and sat on the couch facing the TV. They sat there together, completely silent, until the end of *The National*. Ideas for her novel whirled in her mind. She felt excited about a scene. Eagerly, she turned to him to see if she could voice her excitement, her thoughts. The jagged plane of his face, the full drooping mouth and grey eyes darting from the book to the TV to the book again clearly did not acknowledge her presence. She sighed. She was childish to think the world was made to entertain her.

They went to bed after performing the evening ritual of turning off lights, checking to see if the doors were locked, looking in on the children, waiting for the other to finish in the bathroom. In bed, his body smelled of alcohol. She turned her face towards the open door and breathed in the hallway air.

"Good God, Jason, it's four o'clock in the morning!" Don screamed like a shrew. "I have to get up for work in two hours!" Looking like a Sumo wrestler in his shorts, he picked up the child and gave him a resounding whack. Robin's heart raced. She wanted to stop him but she didn't know how. Obedience had been pounded on her when she was a child and her marriage vows had that dreaded word in it. She had been a dutiful wife for seven years. At each hit, she thought back to when it all first started. Had it not begun when Lyn was born? Was it not just the classic sibling rivalry stage? Was this really necessary? She used to cry helplessly in another room whenever Don was at it. She leapt up now and followed them.

"Not the head, Don," her voice trembled. Whenever Don hit Jason on the head, his favourite target, she felt the jab against her own. "We don't do this back home."

"You're in Canada now," Don yelled, looking white and big. He hit the air dismissively with his large hand and shoved his way out of Jason's room in disgust.

She stood stunned. Her son had disappeared into his blanket. She wanted to hold him but her own body was shaking uncontrollably. "Not the head," she mumbled stupidly.

She clutched her own now as the student in Levis blew smoke rings towards her.

"He's a great guy," the fourth year honours student said, nodding towards her husband, as the eleven students sat and drank around the living room for the last class of Don's seminar.

The smoke made her eyes smart. She glanced at the pewter beer mug they had honoured him with: Dr Don Blotter, Number One.

"Just great. One of the few profs you can really talk to. Great drinker, too," the levis smiled knowingly as his beer toppled over and spilled on the beige carpet. "You like it here?" he asked her, spilling nuts on the beer spill. She stared at him. "Too small a town for you? I see you pushing the stroller. Kids keep you active?"

Robin wanted to discuss the White Ground lekythoi she had seen in the Ashmolean once but the student only wanted to talk about her sleeping children. What else could a prof's wife know?

She heard a child coughing in a bedroom. Jason. Asthma. The smoke was going up the stairs. She ran up, opened his window and closed his door.

"Mummy. Can't breathe."

She rocked him silently. Her brown shirt smelled of smoke. Her hair smelled of cigarettes.

"Mummy, you're crying."

"It's just once a year. Just once a year. Professor's wife's role. Clean ashtrays. Serve the drinks. Look stupid while they discuss the latest books. What questions do they ask me? How're the kids? You like it here? Every year, the same. Same faces, different names. Same names, different faces. Only younger as I get older. Cleaning ashtrays."

She stopped suddenly. Her poor firstborn. Receiving her negative images. Had she damaged him?

It was the first week of April and the snow was gone but her heart was still winter. Her novel was now being written in her blood. As her sister's life and death formed before her eyes, she saw her own life bleeding away, the afterbirth refusing to come out of the womb. In the office, she grunted, damned, cried over the novel. At home, she was calm and silent, keeping her pain in control.

During the exam weeks when the students' essays built up around Don's recliner chair like the stones of a rising fort, she stayed home. She kept the children out of his way. It was his work that brought home the money, as he was wont to say, and she earned her keep by watching that everything was to his order. Of her own work, her writing, it was assumed that she frittered her time away for no financial gain and upset the family life.

The three weeks away from her writing made her restless. She dropped cups. Don screamed. The children cried. She steeled herself, postponed her desires for harmony at home. When she was calm, Don was benevolent and continued his marking, ignoring the peace and quiet as a God-given right of a hard-working man.

At last the marks were in and she was free again to be defiant. After turning on the portable tape recorder she brought in to the office tonight and as the strains of Edith Piaf's song proclaiming no, no she had no regrets poured into her soul as if she claimed those words for her own, Robin brooded over the finished manuscript. Here it lay, 429 pages, smooth in her palms. She slid her fingers up and down the title page. The feel was exquisite. What if she had lost Don's favour? No matter. Here was the novel, concrete in her hands, words that came together to mean. This was the meaning of her sister's life and death. "Here, Matthew, I give you your mother," she spoke out loud in the dark office, the one light focused on the manuscript. "Know her. This is how she looked, how she talked, how she thought. How she loved you."

Robin remembered: she was rocking Matthew to sleep, her sister was kneeling by the bed, praying the rosary. Once in a while, her sister would look up at them with tears in her eyes. "I can hardly wait till November. To be with Peter again. He's found a house in some small village near La Rochelle. Did I tell you? It was in his letter today. The Army's not paying for it. Just a small house, just right for the three of us. He sent me a picture." She nodded towards the dresser. "On the top near the jewelry box."

Robin put the sleeping Matthew in his crib and picked up the picture. "Will he have to drive to the base every day?"

"Twenty, twenty-five minutes away. He bought an old Morris Minor. After his stint, we can have it shipped back here. What do you think?"

"Small, yes. Less space to clean, anyway. You'll be doing everything. It will be lonely, out in the bush."

"I don't mind. I miss him."

"A year and a half to go before his service is over."

Her sister kissed the cross on the rosary. "I know I've been foolish. Maybe I should have waited, married him after his tour of duty. But I just couldn't wait. I love him so. When you love someone, you just have to be with him."

Robin fingered her manuscript. This was a story for Matthew. This was a life for Matthew. Focus. Not only her sister's but also her own life had focused. Writing was about love; writing was love. Writing was for someone loved. Words were shields to protect the weak. These days, when Don raised his hand, she spoke up in Jason's defence, deflecting Don's curse with her resolve. Her quiet had exploded inside her and now she threw back everything at Don. There would no longer be postponements, suspensions of desires. She would not wait for him to finish an article for a learned journal before she could write her own unscholarly piece. When he flipped the whip, she would not jump.

"It's finished, then?" Her sister came out of *Little Dorrit*.

"It was worth it, wasn't it?"

"Did you learn anything?"

"While everything was in order at home, Don felt good and was kind to us. But when I left things in disarray in order to write, then he whimpered, whined, cursed, assaulted me with a barrage of witty insults usually aimed at the administration. Had I accepted my post meekly, his true character would not have surfaced."

"Hmm. Is that all you learned?"

"No."

"Good. Life besides and death beyond that. This was for Jason, then?"

"This was for Matthew!"

"Ah, Matthew," her sister sighed. "Matthew's mine. Sons and Lovers. Do you remember in San Francisco how I wouldn't let anyone touch him?"

"How can I ever forget? You keep reminding me. How can I ever forget you? You're a daily communion: Do this in remembrance of me. You're an Over and Over. You're driving me mad."

Her sister glided towards a Walter Scott. "Didn't he write himself to death? Don't you be doing that. While you're alive, live!" She faded into *Rob Roy*. "One forgets everything except the vengeance."

It was midnight when Robin finally left the office. As she was locking the door, she heard a door open behind her.

"Hullo!" The man's voice echoed in the dimly lit hallway. "You're out late tonight, aren't you?"

She whirled around, her nerves alerted. She managed a weak hello.

"What do you do in there, night after night, in Professor Bates's office?" He was a tall, slightly balding man dressed in a dark blue all-weather coat.

"Writing. I write." She tried to keep her voice nonchalant. A stalker.

"Ahh," he whispered. "A writer." He kept up with her rapid pace down the steps. "What do you write?"

"Lies. I write lies."

He stared at her for a moment to gauge her seriousness. Then he broke into an easy laugh. "Fiction writer, then."

Not a rapist. Not a murderer. Just someone's husband, another professor, working late in his office, leaving his wife and children to their own affairs, their own agonies. "Yes, fictive truth."

He stopped suddenly. The exit was just within reach. But she was no longer nervous. Just another man. Sons and lovers. She walked ahead, leaving him to his own devices. He followed quickly, gave his name and offered his hand. She smiled and with her novel clutched near her heart, she raced across the campus, legs wobbly but determined to run.

It was May, the grass under her feet determined to grow in spite of everything cruel. The trees were green again. Life was beginning everywhere. Her novel was done. She had discovered all kinds of truths, all kinds of lies. Her eyes could see the veins of leaves. Worms wiggled on the pavement. She entered the house humming no, no regrets. Don called out her name. Surprised that Don should speak to her, she went into the living room cautiously.

"Your people phoned from San Francisco. Matthew—"

Her novel fell on the carpet. "Matthew—" she whispered.

"He's dead. Plane crash."

Chariot

TANYA SELVARATNAM

He came over to this country, he would say, on the s s *Hope*. Along the way, he had stopped in Europe—Belgium, Brussels; Austria, Vienna— until he landed in Lawrence, Massachusetts, a city that now almost doesn't exist except for the factories that stand like ruins beyond the bridge at the city's gate. For many days, he had no home and parked himself at an international students' centre where he made contact via pay phone—when a call was only five cents—with the home of his pen pal. She's now a drunkard. She had a daughter who was born on the same day as his own, and was killed as she walked across a street. He would never fill me in on how exactly this woman came to be his pen pal, but she was there waiting for him at the other end of the phone in her Florida home. He felt at home knowing that he existed so close to this familiar voice.

Two days after he landed in Lawrence, Massachusetts, he befriended a woman with a family of two red-headed daughters. He stayed with them until he went to live at college. During his first winter with snow, he had asked the eldest daughter, "How do you know if your ears are falling off?"

He had come to this country to escape his own, to be free from being the youngest of seven children under a very strict though loving mother, but also to become a doctor, and that he did. He became a doctor who took care of people's sanity because, he claimed, it was the easiest way to become a doctor and because he felt that the underdogs made the world go round.

Later he returned to his country to find a bride, and he brought her back to California, where the weather was more akin to that back home. After this, when his wandering had ceased, he and my mother had me. Something in him changed; he began to curse life over and over again and damned the day he settled down.

It had been a long time in the making: the end of our family. Twenty years to be exact. My parents had tried many times to hasten it along, living apart, taking vows of silence with each other. But the break was never quite final. They always stayed together, claiming one glue: me. They were staying together for me. I knew it was more than that. They couldn't live without each other, or at least couldn't figure out a way to live without each other.

That would all change. In 1979, during one trip to Sri Lanka, the place we come from, an astrologer told my mother that my father would be a widower. Moreover, he was a muttah, a guy who didn't know how good he had it. But this seer also said I would be a doctor. He took our money and disappeared.

Thirteen years later, on another trip to Sri Lanka, my mother found a more accurate teller. First, she went to the third floor of an office building near the capital cemetery. The office was called Janmalokha. She handed a bespectacled elder in grey polyester pants a slip of paper with my father's birth details. The man disappeared into another room and emerged after ten minutes with a two-page computerized chart with all the suns and moons that were rising and all the houses of my father's life. She handed him a two-hundred-rupee note, about four dollars, and then went to a house. It was an old yellow concrete house elevated on a red concrete foundation. She entered a room with only an old wooden desk and three carved wooden chairs. She handed another bespectacled gentleman, but this time wearing a brown sarong, the computer-generated chart. Silently, he pondered it over the top of his glasses. He told my mother there was death in my father's chart. In two years.

That December on Christmas Eve my father got a pain in his chest. He made such a big deal about it, straining and breathing, that we thought he was playing the fool. Upon his insistence, we took him to the emergency room. Doctor said he was fine, but my father, also a doctor, asked for some tests. The next day he got the results. There was a problem, a tumour on his lungs. The day after that he had a biopsy. Two days after that we got the news. He had lung cancer. The week after that, the day following New Year's, one lung was removed. It being the holiday season, many members of our family were in town, so there was a cushion of people to soften the shock of seeing my father rigged up to all those wires and monitors.

His doctor, a man my father had lunched with many a time in the hospital cafeteria, said the size of the removed tumour indicated he had developed the cancer two years ago. If it had not been detected, he would have been dead within three to five months. The doctor said, "Your father's a lucky man." His eyes said something else I couldn't make out. When my father had sufficiently recovered from the shock of losing a lung, he began chemo along with the roller coaster that lasted for exactly two years. Until the very end, we couldn't tell if he was going to live or die; just when he seemed to be on his last leg, he bounced back; and just as he started to relax he would falter. The doctors wouldn't tell us what to expect, because I suspect they're trained in this country not to make predictions or tell the whole truth so that if things don't fan out, as they say, they might get sued.

When my dad came back from the hospital that first time his cancer was confirmed, I looked at his face, saw the tears on my mother's and knew, I just knew it was cancer. I had had a dream four months before that my mother and I were on vacation while my father lay curled up on the floor at home. In the dream, my mother got a call from someone saying, "Dead." And my mother cried, "Daddy has died. Daddy's died. And we're not there."

It was the beginning of Clinton's term. Health care was a word you heard a lot during that first year in office. Somehow you had this vague idea that health care was going to be alright. Well, it killed us. The doctors took care of my father well, and he, being a doctor himself, didn't pay as much as most. But it killed us anyway. Too many weekends at Caesar's Palace left the savings unprepared for the shock of hospital bills, and straying in and out of the dying ward at Long Beach Community left us in between worlds.

Six months after my father was diagnosed, two months after he completed his first of many rounds of chemotherapy, he and my mother visited me in Massachusetts. During the late 1950s, my father was the original Sri Lankan in Massachusetts having arrived on the s s *Hope* from our country, so far away. He loved to visit Massachusetts and was particularly proud that his daughter had ended up living there, away from "the glitzy decrepitude of California." Since his illness, he had become an avid walker and found in Cambridge ample stomping ground. Sometimes I accompanied him, and we'd counter the cleansing effects of our strolls with a large meal.

One day, he wanted lobster, so I took him to the one seafood restaurant in the area. Throughout the day, he had been particularly irritated with my mother, not a hard-to-come-by feeling, but an unjust one nonetheless. To him on that day she couldn't do anything right. The coffee was too bitter; her very speech inspired barks; her nightgown smelled. Distant as my relationship with my mother was, I stood up for her whenever he lashed out at her or cut her out.

She came up at the restaurant. "Your mother is impossible." "And you're not," I said in a firm but still jocular tone. He took instant cover. "Have I ever done wrong by you?" "No, but, oh, we've all fucked up somehow." "I haven't," he said insistently. This was always a difficult game to play with my father; sometimes he was the most self-deprecating human being, other times the most self-denying. And you could never tell which way he'd blow. "Uh . . . what?!" I was hoping to make us agree by joking about our own blackguarded ways. But he wasn't having it.

We started building laundry lists of all the terrible things we had done. Mine involved skipping classes and cavorting with ill-looking men—"losing your credibility," he said. His involved gambling—even more incessantly since he found out he had cancer, at the rate of a thousand dollars a day—keeping an apartment on the beach and hanging out with hideous-looking blonde women with names like Sandy, entertaining a reviled and renowned whore named Ingrid in a ridiculous gold lamé gown in our family home, lying about having attended Woodstock and being a hipster in Nashville (where he did actually live), beating the shit out of my mother, etc. Other than that I had always felt he was an excellent father, never raised his fist to me, never shouted, never judged, always enlightening on issues of life and well-being—he was a psychiatrist after all. Our meal was over. He quickly paid the bill, and we abandoned our twin lobster tails. I lied and said I was going to the library. He didn't even say goodbye and took off down a side street; more walking.

I went straight back to my apartment where my mother was watching Oprah. "Where's Daddy?" she asked, peering from beneath her over-sized pink rimmed glasses that made her look an awful lot like Heather Matarazzo in *Welcome to the Dollhouse*.

"I don't know. He's walking. We had a fight."

"What?"

"I told him he was a shit."

"My god, why did you do that? Always, something happens . . ."

Yes, something always did happen in our family, but we were all strong as bulls and never gave way completely. So much to be thankful for, but for our madness, which was rumoured to be in our genes.

Of all the many memories left behind from those last two years with my father, the last week of his life is the most vivid. My mother called me to say that Daddy was in the hospital, but I didn't need to come. I was in New York. But I had a dream. It was so vague I can't remember the contents, but it gave me the feeling I should go.

I went straight from L A airport to the hospital. Random brown people, other Sri Lankans, were milling around in the hall by my father's room. He was in a special ward for people who were on their last leg. A black girl with sickle-cell anemia was moaning in a room up the hall. She was only fourteen years old. Nobody was visiting her today. Occasionally, a relative would stop by, and there'd be silence in her room, no talking. And maybe she was fighting hard, but she wouldn't scream or cry either. Right next door was a man in the last stages of AIDS. My mother said he'd been in and out of this ward for the past year. He would walk around accompanied by his portable IV stand and smoke cigarettes in the garden. He was always smiling, and his teeth dominated his emaciated face. In another room, I could make out a tiny white-haired woman with her eyes perpetually closed. I figured she was just old. Walking down the hall to my father's room was like rowing down the Styx.

My mother said that my father's pen pal had come from Florida to visit him the day before. She had gotten drunk and wept over him. She was so twisted she wanted to take pictures with my dad. He looked like death kept alive with his skinny frame, bald head, and tubes all up his nose and around his arms. She got her pictures and then rode off to the airport.

The day after I arrived, a doctor came to the waiting room where I sat with my mother. He was whispering to her. Daddy had told him he was dying. "I'm dying, Doc." Each day after that became a routine. Standing outside his room, sitting by his bedside, watching the monitor for his heartbeat, watching him sleep and breathe—one breath, one long breath, one short breath, one heavy breath, one syncopated breath. Some nights, always at night, he was totally alert.

One of those days, I went to the record store to buy his favourite tapes: Nina Simone and Charles Aznavour. I also bought a lobster. I cooked it at home, arranged it on a plate with a ramekin of drawn butter and a side of broccoli. I wrapped the plate up in tin foil, grabbed the tapes and a portable tape player, and my mother drove me to the hospital. Daddy was awake when I got to his room. He glanced down at the lobster and smiled. I put the Aznavour tape on.

"Softer," he said. "Have a bite."

"No, it's for you," I told him, but he couldn't eat.

"Don't you have to go to the car and get the anachronism."

He was speaking rubbish. His mind was melting, and he was far away. He scrunched his face like a child who didn't understand why he couldn't go out and play. He dissolved into his pillow and looked up. "Amma, take me away. Amma is coming." Now I was getting frightened. He never mentioned his mother. She had been killed fourteen years before. We received the news by telephone one day. My mother's mother called. At first, she said Archi (as a Tamil paternal grandmother was called) had fallen on her head and died quickly. No suffering. That same day, it came out that she had been ambushed by thirty men) all Sinhalese) in her home late at night.

Bats hung in the back room of her house. Her daughter was visiting from Australia and hid in the closet while Archi was being hacked to death. Archi had gone to reason with the men. She thought they were robbers. They were killers, with axes, knives, sticks. Not a thing in the house was touched, not the jewelry, not the statues of Jesus, Mary, Joseph, and St Bernadette that stood on a ledge on the wall. But they chopped off Archi's nose, slit her throat, beat her, then vanished.

The daughter was still in the closet, weeping, unaware of what awaited her in the living room. Mary, who had worked for Archi for fifty years, through the birth and growth of six children, stood by the body. She had seen the whole thing. The men didn't touch Mary. She was Sinhalese and a witness. The daughter came out of the closet, got to the door of the living room, where her mother's body lay. She screamed like there was no end to suffering, but scream while you have the strength. On the window were metal bars that Archi had just reluctantly had installed. These bars were to protect her, a lonely widow living with a lonely old maid. The men came through the front door.

My father had heard this tale, and he cried. Now, for the first time, I saw in his face how hard he'd been fighting to live. All these years, he'd tried to be good, but he couldn't be; he'd tried to love, but it didn't work, and now he had no choice. My mother said we should let him sleep.

The next morning, my mother and I showered and drove to the hospital. Daddy was sitting up in bed, perkier than we were and very very clean-smelling, like a baby doused with baby cologne after a bath.

"Guess what happened?" he asked.

"What?" I said, totally bewildered. What could happen to a man with a death sentence, fluid bursting through his distended belly, legs unable to walk.

"I shat in my pants."

He said it with such glee that I giggled. He then recounted how he'd been dreaming about the time he was a child in Sri Lanka. He remembered a hippopotamus that floated in the lake beside his house. He was pissing in the lake on his way home from school; he'd heard about the monster that lived in the lake. He saw it with his very own eyes; he saw it, and it was silent. He threw a stick at it, but it didn't move. He said, "Hallo," and it opened its mouth, and with a rich throaty sound, it mooed. Then, he woke up with an incredible urge to pee. He struggled out of his bed towards the porta-potty wheelchair a few feet away. His legs gave way, he had miscalculated. Diarrhea came pouring forth from his innards. The nurses found him on the floor in a pool of shit. They cleaned him, bathed him with wet towels, and placed him back in bed.

Within two days, he died. I had relieved my mother from her bedside vigil and she went home to shower. Fifteen minutes after she left, he stopped breathing. I didn't notice at first. I was reading *People* to give me something to do, something that wouldn't take any brainpower. Then I realized I wasn't hearing his deep phlegmy breaths. I walked up to him and leaned over. I saw his chest was not moving, looked at his eyes. They opened for a second. I tried to read them. Blank. And his mouth, which had been open before so he could breathe, opened wider. The phlegm gurgled in his throat. Then he died like a balloon dies. His body made a quick and slight move forward. He was gone.

I went out to the waiting room where there was a telephone and called my mother. I said, "Daddy died, but it's okay." She screamed, "What?. . . Couldn't he wait? God is wicked. God is wicked." She said this over and over again. She had gone home for just an hour's respite, and in that hour he decided to take his leave. Funny how the dying can plan this way.

Two weeks later my mother and I travelled to Sri Lanka with his ashes in a heavy copper box. In the capital cemetery, we buried him with his mother who'd been murdered fourteen years before. At my mother's parents' home, at the bottom of an old trunk, I found a bag filled with papers. They were a series of letters from my father written to my mother before they got married and went to hell. My grandmother had saved all these notes, all this time.

November 8, 1968
My Darling Baby,

It seems a long time since I heard from you. I know I am delinquent in writing more often than this, but unfortunately I am so busy with work and studies that it becomes quite impossible to write every day. Nevertheless my love is stronger towards you and in spite of everything, I think of you every day. The weather is . . . becoming colder now, in fact I won't be surprised if it does not begin to snow pretty soon. I understand how you felt when you visited the accident room to see your brother. But when you see quite a few, you don't have the time to get emotionally involved. I spend 2 days a week in the emergency room and we get all sorts of cases. Yesterday a woman came in with most of her body burnt. She is an alcoholic and lives alone. She apparently was smoking a cig in bed and fell asleep. Another case came with attempted suicide. He cut his throat with a knife. All we can do is patch up and hope for the best. At first I too was like you. I kept asking the why and why nots of human behaviour but later on one realizes there are no good answers for the tragedies and degradations of human lives. One accepts the good and the bad and hope that in the near future the good will eventually overwhelm the bad. I also miss you an awful lot and keep dreaming constantly about you. Oh I wish you . . . to me instead of this letter to communicate my thoughts to you. Sometimes I am all alone with the beatings of my heart and that is the time I miss you most. We will definitely have a most happy marriage and nothing on earth will stop us. It will be a most happy one. How are things at Grove Place? I don't know my mother's birthday. Why don't you ask her. We never did ask her. Is your sister having a birthday party? I haven't been to any mixers lately. Hope things are fine and dandy in Ceylon.

Lots of love and kisses and miss you very much.

*

Late tonight, a special on Raymond Carver was on public television, and my father came alive. When he got a perm, when his belly ballooned, when he lost control, and when he lost 20 grand, not exactly in that order. The letter that he wrote me when I went away to school—I think I cried, but I think I was also pissed off. I remember when we saw a friend of the family sitting with a hooker on the tier below us at the Circus Maximus Showroom at Caesar's Palace. I was angry and wanted to go up to him and say, "Does your wife know? And, by the way, your wig is crooked." I always wondered if my father had done the same as he. I remember when Daddy laid his head on my shoulder and cried. His wedding pictures were scattered on the orange carpet that went from my parents' bedroom, by the study, by my bedroom, to the wood floor that framed the front door. He had torn all those pictures up.

The next time I saw him so close, he died. Years from now, I'll recall the image of my father shitting in his pants and telling me about his shitting in his pants. With this image, I remember him fondly. With this image, I remember him and sometimes cry. He was fifty-three when he died, though he always had one foot out of the door of life. There's a saying that originated in China: At thirty, you can stand on your own two feet. At forty, you have no more confusion. At fifty, you know your fate.

The Foreigners

ANITA RAU BADAMI

Mir Alam shook his head and sighed. The newspaper held nothing but news of violence and disaster. Yesterday it was a terrorist bombing in a crowded market in Delhi and today more than a hundred people killed in the agitation over the mosque-temple issue in Rangarh village just outside Lucknow. Some local politician had pointed to a stone which stood beside a small mosque and claimed it was all that remained of a temple built in the fourteenth century and destroyed by Muslim invaders. "Were Hindus going to sit back and let this act of violence against their gods go unprotested?" demanded the minister. "Were they going to meekly remain silent as their land was eaten up by foreigners? There used to be a temple on this spot and now there is a mosque, isn't that an injustice?" And sure as cows give milk, tempers went flying and before you knew it people were out on the streets flinging rocks and country bombs, killing, looting, raping.

You live in a country all your life, six or seven generations of your family were born and died on this same soil and overnight some unscrupulous rascal decides that you are a foreigner, thought Mir Alam ruefully. Nobody had even heard of the wretched village till the politician rogue decided to stir up trouble. That seemed to be the favoured method of collecting votes these days. The old British tactic of divide and rule. Mir Alam sighed again. Human beings could not exist without strife, it seemed. Sikhs and Hindus, Bengalis and Assamese, Tamils and Sri Lankans all fighting and killing each other. Did they forget that they were all humans in the end with the same feelings and emotions and fragile bodies that could so easily be destroyed? So what if they had different gods—only the names were different after all. Mir Alam had thought that after the horrors following the partition of India and Pakistan people would come to their senses, stop all this useless fighting and killing and nonsense. He was only ten when Partition took place, but he carried in the dark recesses of his memory ugly images of that time. The severed head of an unknown boy lying in the drain behind their house. His own mother silent and terrified, clutching him and his sisters while angry fists thumped on their front door. And the sounds of horror that punctured the unnatural silence filling the normally busy street. He had watched his father being beaten up by people he did not even know. They might all have died then if not for their Hindu and Sikh neighbours who had hidden them in their homes. Mir Alam wondered what he would do if trouble erupted again. Then you could at least trust your neighbours to help you. But now there were so many new people around and Mir Alam hardly knew any of them. His old friends had all gone one by one; Mohammed Shaikh the doctor who had kept the death god away from his patients for so many years had been finally claimed himself; Quadir Musa with his oldest son in Bombay—he still sent a postcard every Id; and Gyan Nath, the pandit-ji with a tidbit of wisdom for everyone and food for every beggar who stopped at his door, killed on his way back from Dehradun when the bus overturned on a curve. Poor Gyan, he was a good man and a loyal friend. All gone, all gone. Jayant Bhai was still in the large stone house a few blocks away, in the Hindu neighbourhood. After Partition, it seemed to Mir Alam, even towns and cities had split up into clearly defined *religious* zones. Hindus here, Christians there, Muslims somewhere else.

Jayant Bhai was one of the people whose family had helped Mir Alam's in times of trouble. The two of them used to meet often at the Regal Tea Palace every Saturday to exchange news and discuss the state of the world, but since his son entered politics Jayant Bhai kept to himself.

"Arrey Mir Alam," he said the last time they met. "I tell you, never write your property over to your children while you have breath in your body. They will take your money and your mind, your home and your conscience. Look at me, do I have a say in anything since my son took over our lives? I might as well be dead, I would be *happier* dead." Jayant Bhai was bitter about his son's rabid political stance and had blurted out his unhappiness one evening when Mir Alam bumped into him in the vegetable market. "There was a time when politicians worked for the country. Nowadays, the country is there to be looted by these *goondas* who stand for election. I know what I say is true, I am ashamed to say it, but I have a *goonda* in my own home, Mir Alam, in my very own home!"

Well, thought Mir Alam, scanning the newspaper again, it looked like Jayant Bhai's *goonda* son was leading a procession today down this very road. A peaceful procession, said the newspaper, to protest past atrocities against Hindus in a country that rightfully belonged to them, in a country that had always welcomed foreigners of every faith. (Mir Alam winced at the word *foreigners*. Is that how people felt about him, that he was a firang like the British and the French and the Portuguese?) There was a photograph of Jayant Bhai's son waving a righteous fist, his plump lips pursed, a garland of roses around his neck. When did the boy become a religious fanatic? Mir Alam remembered him as a polite child with serious eyes, good at his studies, a year or two younger than his own Ahmed. It was amazing how a seed that you thought was good could grow into a twisted tree. The newspaper cautioned people to remain inside their homes as far as possible just in case there was violence, although the organizers of the *morcha* had promised they would make sure things stayed calm.

Mir Alam leaned down from his balcony and called to Tika Ram the grocer who rented the store below. "Tika Ramji," he called, "are you there? Have you heard about this *morcha* that Jayant Bhai's son is taking out?"

Tika Ram's assistant answered. "He is also in the *morcha*, Mir sahib. But he has told me to close the shop down at ten o'clock in case there is any *gol-mal*."

"But what *gol-mal* are they expecting? I thought this was going to be peaceful. That is what the papers said."

"A thousand crazy people marching down the road, a by-election less than a month away, and you believe the newspapers! Arrey *miyan*, which world are you living in? This place is like a tin full of kerosene waiting for a lighted match to blow it all up. If I were you I would sit quietly inside my house with all the doors and windows locked and barred."

Mir Alam drew his head in, feeling disturbed. Especially by the fact that his tenant was also a part of this procession. He had not seemed the sort of person who went crazy over religious matters. In fact they had had the occasional discussion on god and come to the agreement that god existed in a man's heart and that was all that mattered. So when had Tika Ram changed his views? Mir Alam could not understand the speed with which things changed around him. Why, even old buildings that had formed familiar and comforting landmarks disappeared overnight to be replaced by high-rise apartments grey and featureless with dozens of flimsy matchbox-size homes where entire families crammed themselves and their belongings. They came and they went, the new migrant population that had become a part of every city in the country. No stability, no long-term friendships, nothing. Why, if there was anyone he could truly call a friend now, it was only the English mem, Edith Johnson. A *firang* woman from another country, that too! (Although, it must be admitted, even she had been acting very strange of late, *very* strange). Mir Alam leaned back in his easy chair and reflected that perhaps the only friends he really had were his pigeons. They might have brains the size of peas but what did it matter? Human beings for all their mighty brains were idiots after all.

"Turr-turr-tuturr" burbled the pigeons that Mir Alam kept on his terrace. They strutted and dipped, fanned out their tails and perched coquettishly on the swirling wrought-iron railing that hemmed the large balcony suspended one storey above the ground.

"Ah my pretty one, here . . . here . . . something nice for you," murmured Mir Alam, his thatch of grey hair matching the bird's plumage almost exactly. He spread a thin layer of grain on the floor and watched fondly as the pigeons pecked and stabbed and marched around in little circles like Victorian matriarchs with their corsetted chests thrust out. "Ey Rani my darling, what a beauty you are," he crooned, rubbing the back of his forefinger gently on the head of a pure white pigeon. "And you, my precious Moti, aren't you a clever one?" A grey bird cocked its head attentively and looked at the old man with pink-rimmed eyes.

Mir Alam leaned back in his easy chair, its striped cloth faded from the fierce light of the sun. It was his favourite chair and no amount of nagging from his wife Roshan would make him consign it to the dustbin. He flung another handful of grain at the birds, smiling at their excited fluttering. The old man enjoyed Sundays when he could wake up early and talk to his pigeons instead of rushing to catch the Number 40 bus, elbowing through the tight-packed crowd, squeezing his way out when his stop arrived, trying to ignore angry glares from militant young women who thought that he was groping at their bodies.

"Arrey Baba," he wanted to reassure them, "I am too old for all that nonsense, and besides, I am only trying to get out of this bus before the stupid driver takes off."

The driver, a young muscular fellow with a ferocious moustache and the reek of cheap liquor hanging over him like a dank fog, took a perverse pleasure in starting the bus suddenly, before any of his passengers had alighted, roaring with laughter as they cursed and jumped recklessly off the accelerating vehicle. Poor, foolish man to find happiness in tormenting others! Up until a few years ago, Mir Alam used to ride to work on his scooter, a ramshackle vehicle which had transported his wife to the market and both of them back with all their shopping. The roads were emptier then, he was certain of that although Roshan insisted that he was merely imagining these things. "The roads were just as crowded," she teased him. "You were younger, that's the difference!"

It was true though, that the new road running past his house had cut the time taken to cover the distance to the downtown area of the city by half and so the whole world preferred this route. What was once a quiet residential street had become a major highway, or so it seemed. It was good for Mir Alam in a way, his house was now prime property and he had no problem finding tenants for the shops on the ground floor. They, in turn, found their businesses booming and paid their rents on time. The noise was unbearable, but then every coin had two sides to it, the good and the bad, so no use grumbling. However, taking the scooter to work was nightmarish, Mir Alam preferred the relative safety of the bus. Nobody in their right minds tried to overtake a Lucknow bus with its maniacal drivers, each of whom thought that he was a film star.

Especially after that fellow in South India—Rajnikant, a bus conductor—made it big in films, all these drivers thought that they were heroes riding horses!

By the time Mir Alam reached the grey Public Works Department building where he worked as a senior clerk, his starched white shirt was a mess of lines and creases, and he trailed a faint odour of sweat and hair oil.

"Salaam Miyan, and how are you?" he said punctiliously to each of the row of clerks hunched over their papers like ostriches absorbed in the sand, working his way to his desk at the far end of the musty cavernous office. There he would sit for the rest of the day, before his ancient Remington typewriter, which had a worn out "e" key so that it looked like a "c," typing memos and letters beginning with "Dear Sir or Madam" (he could remember an era when it was only Dear Sir), and ending with "your humble servant," or, if obsequiousness was not called for, a crisp "yours sincerely'.

*

In the small suite of rooms across the landing from Mir Alam's home, Edith Johnson leaned almost into the yellowish mirror on her dressing table and traced a shaky line of lipstick across a mouth as crinkled as an old carnation, darkened her pale lashes with clotted mascara several years old and kept fluid with so many drops of water that there was barely any colour left now; she drew two uneven arches where her eyebrows used to be (till she allowed that wretched girl in the beauty parlour to thread them for her) and rubbed rouge on to a cheekbone. Her attention was distracted momentarily by the flutter of wings outside her window and she forgot to rouge the other cheek.

"Dratted birds," she muttered. "How many times do I have to remind Mir Alam to keep his wretched creatures away from my window."

Edith hated the pigeons. She couldn't understand why her old friend took it into his head to breed *pigeons* of all things. Dogs, cats, even fish she could forgive. But not these noisy, smelly birds which fluttered in and out of her rooms, leaving their droppings on her windowsills, feathers on the floor, a stink in the still air of the rooms. She couldn't even keep her windows open anymore, and in this Lucknow heat her life without any ventilation was intolerable.

Mir Alam wouldn't listen to her complaints either. He just laughed and said, "Arrey Edith-ji, what do you have against these innocent birds hanh? They don't come inside my house, so why should they enter yours?"

He dismissed her protests as if she were a senile old bat or a fussy child. Edith was beginning to get really angry. She had even tried complaining to Roshan, who was so much more reasonable than Mir Alam. But Roshan just shook her head. "That man is stubborn. He has never listened to anyone and the more you tell him the more pigeons he will buy. I tell you Edith, I nearly had a pigeon fall into my cooking the other day and the silly man tells me, *me* to be careful, if you please! Just ignore him and he will forget his pigeons after a while."

At first there was only one pigeon and Edith did not really mind it. Then came another and a third and now there were twenty-five, maybe more, crooning and mumbling every minute of the day. What was worse was the smell of feathers and droppings—a ripe odour of mossy water and whitewash that had permeated every particle of air in her home. And it was at its worst on Sundays when Mir Alam sat in his balcony and encouraged the birds to flap and flutter around. For Edith, Sundays had always been a day to look forward to—when Roshan made biryani and invited her over. The small ritual had started when Mir Alam's daughters were young and Edith had offered to coach them on the weekend, help with their homework if they needed it. And after the girls got married and left, Roshan continued to have her over.

As the first aroma of basmati rice rose, crept into her house and mingled slowly with the smell of tender frying mutton and delicate hints of coriander, coconut, cumin and clove, Edith's stomach rumbled and she waited eagerly for Roshan to knock on her door, as she had done for so many years, and call, "Eedith, Principal Miss, come, come, food is ready."

And Edith, waiting like a child promised a treat, would allow an interval of five minutes or so for decency's sake, before crossing the landing. Now even that simple pleasure was blighted by Mir's pigeons. The appetizing smell of the biryani was tinged with pigeon-shit stink. Edith had tried talking to Mir Alam about the pigeons as Roshan had suggested.

"They make a mess, Mir Alam," she told him. "I wish you would do something."

Mir Alam had just laughed, the old fool. "Arrey Edith Miss, what do you want me to do? Build them a toilet perhaps?"

"I don't like the way they smell."

"What smell, Principal Miss? My pretty ones don't smell. It must be that drain down there. How many times I have told these corporation fellows. But those *ulloo ke patthey*, when have they ever listened?"

"It's not the drain, it's your damn birds," insisted Edith.

Mir Alam pursed his lips to register his annoyance and refused to say anything more. For a week he did not speak to Edith to show her how much she had offended him but she was not in the least impressed. Men! They had no idea how childish they were. The pigeons were pests and that was that. If Mir Alam wasn't going to do something about them, she was. Especially now that they had started migrating to her balcony *en masse* in the afternoon just when she was taking her nap. Their constant cooing drove her crazy and when they flew away in the evening, they left a mess of white streaks all over the railing and on her windows. She couldn't even hang out clothes to dry and her house reeked of damp underwear. Perhaps she could frighten the wretched creatures away. She wandered around the house looking for her comb, muttering to herself. Her eyes fell on a box of firecrackers that she had purchased during Diwali last year for Roshan's grandchildren who came home for the festival holidays from Delhi. They were tiny red ones strung together and looked like railway tracks. They made a tremendous noise, almost like gunshots and would be perfect to scare the birds away without harming them. Although, the way Edith felt, she would willingly kill the pigeons. She grinned to herself and touched the crackers. Yes, yes. A couple of bangs and no more pigeons. Perhaps. Did birds have long memories? Would their fear stay with them and prevent them from invading her space again?

Edith slipped on her yellow and white silk dress, pleased that it still fitted her. Baba Tailors, whose shop downstairs was now a television repair shop, had stitched it for her twenty-five years ago, faithfully copying the pattern from a British women's magazine that Edith had pinched from the Army Officers' Club. She remembered how naughty, how utterly sinful she felt as she stuffed the magazine into the waist of her stockings, hidden under the flowing green dress she wore that day. Natalie Cross had caught her at it in the Ladies Room, but was too drunk to remember it later. She had giggled and remarked in a stage whisper, "Caught you with your fingers in your knickers darling. Don't worry, shan't tell a soul that I found the little schoolteacher tickling herself!"

Natalie was always drunk. She drank to blot out the heat and the noise, the dust and the unending variety of insects and diseases, the subterranean hostility she could feel running like a tremor through the crowds of brown faces around her but could not see. She drank to the memory of a small island that she had left behind as a girl for a warm, moist country that made her feel nauseated and headachy more often than she cared to think about. Natalie, like so many before her, came as a young bride, married to a man who believed that he was working the mother lode here in this barely tolerable place, that he was on the path to fame and fortune. She had thought she would return to England after a few years with improbably large diamonds in her ears, with enough money to buy a mansion, a title, and admission into homes and clubs hitherto closed to them because they were not rich or pedigreed enough.

Edith, on the other hand, had come to India because she could not stand the English air anymore, or the tiny brownstone she shared with her savage father, straight out of a cruel Dickensian world, her tuberculous mother whose blood-stained spittle stained every sheet and pillow in the house, and her four brothers who were well on their way to becoming quite as monstrous as their father. She thought anything was better than her world and India with its aura of romance and the unknown beckoned. Perhaps she would meet one of those dashing British officers one read about in magazine romances and marry him, escape forever this wretched life. She was drawn to that distant land for much the same things that persuaded other immigrants to leave the familiar and embark on trips across uncharted waters—the desire for a new and better life, the belief that there was a fortune to be made elsewhere, the call of adventure, or to put it in more pedestrian terms, because the grass on the other side of the fence appeared to be so much more lush and inviting.

A job as governess to Mrs Harold Milne's three horrid children brought her to Madras Presidency where she met Ronnie Chambers the dashing young soldier she had hoped to encounter. Enamoured by him, she abandoned Mrs Milne and moved to Lucknow along with Ronnie only to have her hopes of marriage extinguished as soon as he laid eyes on an elegant young woman with an inheritance to match her looks, which made her distinctly more attractive to a man on the make than Edith who had nothing more than a nice smile and a good figure to recommend her. She found no time to regret Ronnie, for almost immediately she started teaching history at St Dominic's, a new school in this antique town with its crumbling palaces and courteous old ways. Nobody, not even the sour-tempered butcher, it appeared to Edith, could utter a word without first prefacing it with a polite phrase. One of the army wives fixed the job for her—in India, Edith found, everything was fixable. The name of the woman was lost in the dusty drawers of memory, but she did remember a plump smiling face, a mass of grey curls, a busybody involved in all kinds of charitable works. The new school was her pet project. She knew the principal from one of her husband's previous postings—Allahabad, or Kanpur or something, and was actively engaged in recruiting teachers. Edith, she insisted, would simply adore teaching at St Dominic's. She brushed aside Edith's mild protests that she knew nothing of History.

"Pah," she said, "you just need to read stuff out from books about wars and kings and all that. What's so difficult about it? And such a good salary too. Don't be a silly girl now and do say yes."

And so Edith packed her small trunk and moved out of Ronnie's guest house to an apartment in Old Hyder Ganj. It had been quite a pretty area then, with a few respectable British families scattered among the largely Muslim population. The important thing was that she was close to the school, just a five-minute ride in a rickshaw. The place she rented was not really an apartment so much as a suite of rooms spread across the upper storey of a large whitewashed building. The lower floor was let out to a row of shopkeepers—a grocer, a tailor, two musicians, and a halwai who started cooking his sugary confections at three in the morning to sweeten the tongues, as he put it, of the surly stream of truckers, construction workers and other people whose day started earlier than most. Edith took the apartment for the view from her bedroom. In the morning she could see the sun slip out of its envelope of darkness and set fire to the Gomti River unravelling slowly through fields matted with watermelon and pumpkin vines. Thin wisps of mist drifted away from the bulky domes of ancient palaces now partially obscured by a multistoreyed apartment building in which the lower flats had been occupied even though the building was incomplete. A lattice of iron girders still encased it like a cage and the topmost storeys were empty shells with only outer walls and a few of the support walls inside. Edith had heard that the buyers were mainly people who worked in the Gulf and had bought flats here as an investment. The builders, taking advantage of the absence of the buyers, used the money for other projects, or to build their own mansions, leaving each new building unfinished after a certain height. If the owners came home unexpectedly, there were a million excuses that could be used—building permits not approved, workers' strike, truck strike, cement shortage, electricity failures, no water, whattodo sir, this is India.

Before the pigeons blighted her life, Edith would sit on her balcony every morning with a cup of coffee and watch the world pass by on the street below. There was something to see everyday, a procession, a festival, a fight. She knew some of the people who went by, for she had taught them a long time ago. There were sounds that never seemed to change. The clangour of rickshaw cycles—poinka, poinka, poinka; the woman with her basket of fresh greens, the fellow who sold brooms and buckets and sharpened knives. Edith wondered vaguely why she hadn't heard any of them today, though. It wasn't as if they took Sundays off. Neither could they all be ill! Perhaps today was some festival she had forgotten about, there were so many in this country that she often lost track. She glanced out of her window. Odd, even the usual throng of loafers and ne'er-do-wells who loitered near the sweetmeat shop was missing. In fact, the road was far too quiet, a waiting sort of quiet. What on earth was going on? She must remember to ask Roshan and Mir Alam when she went over. They would know.

When the British left the country, Edith elected to stay behind. She had lost touch with her family in England, most of them, except for her older brother's daughter who wrote brief letters every Christmas. Edith wasn't sure that she was doing the right thing by staying here. She was still a foreigner in this country after all and not a particularly popular one. She decided to give herself another year to make up her mind. In the meantime, she wrote to her niece and asked her to keep a lookout for a small property on the outskirts of London. She would be able to afford that out of her savings. The niece dutifully enclosed details of reasonably priced houses, near London and in the country, every year along with her Christmas missive, but when Edith did not reach a decision on any of them, she stopped sending the advertisements and clippings. The years drifted by and the desire to return to England, never too insistent to begin with, faded away completely. Mir Alam did not ask her to move, not even when his children were grown up and their own home became so crowded the son had to sleep in the living room. He did not even raise the rent. This apartment with its heavy furniture, its crimson curtains which allowed the sun to filter in dimly and give the rooms a red tinge so that Edith felt that she was living in a bottle of ruby-red Rooh Afzah sherbet, this was her home and there was no going back. She was too old to settle in another country even if it was the country where she was born. Now if only Mir Alam would be a little more reasonable about the pigeons.

Edith peered out of her window again to see if the street below had gone back to normal.There was still no sign of the loiterers or any of the itinerant vendors. There were two or three policemen though, leaning against their bicycles and sipping cups of tea from earthen containers. And winding down the road was a crowd of people, chanting something she could not hear properly, waving flags and banners. Every now and then a few of the people in the crowd shouted slogans and danced around in small circles.The crowd stretched back several kilometres down the road and moved slowly.

Something was going on here. "Policeman-ji," she called waving her hand at one of the fellows sipping tea down below. The man looked up and grinned. "Good-marning Principal Miss, how you are?"

Edith remembered the face vaguely, but not the name. "What is going on? Where is everybody? Some problem expected?"

"There is a procession coming down this road Miss-ji. No trouble, but."

"If there is no trouble why are you policemen down there?"

"Arrey Miss-ji," replied the policeman. "They said no trouble, but better to be prepared, that's what we say. The procession is Hindu, this is a Muslim area, so who can say what will happen?"

Edith pulled her head back in. Well, she better not step out today, not even to buy some more embroidery thread for the cushion covers she had started last month. She limped to her dressing table mirror again to make sure that her bra strap or her slip wasn't showing. She was particular about these little details although she was only going next door. She noticed the unrouged cheek and tutted to herself. Well if she wasn't getting completely absentminded! She'd forget to wear her underwear one of these days if she did not watch out. Edith smoothed her hands affectionately over her silk dress and twirled around once like a young girl. She was about to move away when there was a flutter of wings. A pigeon flew in through the open window of her bedroom and settled cheekily on the ceiling fan. She had forgotten to shut it after speaking to the policeman. Damn! Another followed and then another. Edith limped around the room waving her arms. "*Shooshooshoo!* Get out!" she shouted furiously. The birds erupted overhead in a flutter of feathers, blind with panic. They shat on Edith's clean white hand-embroidered bedspread (a farewell gift from the teachers at school when she had retired), making her even more furious. She flung open more windows and tried to shoo the birds towards them. They fluttered into her kitchen and a few more came in through the windows. The smell of bird entered Edith's nostrils and drove her crazy. She yanked the balcony door open, kicking at it to get it unstuck where it had swollen up with monsoon moisture. The balcony was alive with pigeons, hundreds of them, it seemed to Edith. She could see Mir Alam's slippered feet resting on the railings of his balcony next door and the sight only incensed her further. Stubborn old fool, sitting there calm as you please. She would teach him and his pigeons a lesson. Edith hobbled inside again and fished out a string of firecrackers. She laid them out on the balcony and lit a match. Then she shut the door and clamped her hands over her ears.

*

The procession was now chanting its way past the house. Mir Alam, like other people on the street watched with idle curiosity, reassured by the presence of the policemen that this was going to remain a peaceful event. Inside the house, he could hear Roshan humming to herself as she added the final touches to the biryani which he could smell and wondered whether there were any mangoes left in the refrigerator. This summer the mango crop had been extraordinary—the intense heat had filled the trees with the honeysweet fruit. Ah yes, he would ask Roshan to cut a few langras for dessert. He preferred the subtlety of a dussehri but it didn't matter, a mango was a mango no matter what kind. Mir Alam rose to go inside his house when the first firecracker went off, loud and sharp in the torpid summer air, cutting across the sound of the procession below. Then another and another. The old man looked around uncertainly, wondering whether someone had been shot. The crowd on the street stopped chanting and somebody screamed, "We are being attacked. Run!"

There was complete pandemonium. Another voice shouted, "The Muslims are shooting. We are being attacked by the Mussulmans."

Some more of the crackers went off in Edith's balcony. The crowd below exploded and several people at the head of the procession picked up stones. A man in a red shirt flung a brick at the store window below and yelled, "Arrey, see that's where the shots are coming from—that Mussalman's house. Go back where you came from!"

"Circumcised bastards!" yelled another man rushing towards Mir Alam's door. "*Haramzaadey*! Go back! Go back! This is Ram Rajya, Hindus allowed only!"

Mir Alam sank into his easy chair. He recognized the man battering on his front door. It was Jayant Bhai's son, whom he had known as a boy this high, who had celebrated Diwali and Id with his own two sons, and now . . .

"Go back where?" he wanted to ask. "Can one travel back in time or in history?" He was too old now to feel the fear that he had felt years ago when, as a child, he had heard the same cries tearing the air, felt the waves of rage which left in its wake the stench of blood and burnt flesh. Above his head feathers eddied and swirled as his pigeons flew in panic from Edith's balcony back to the sanctuary of his own.

He leaned over the balcony railing and called to the man who was rapidly being surrounded by the incensed crowd. "Arrey, son of Jayant Bhai," he said. "What is happening, beta? Why are you breaking my door down? You want to come in, wait a minute na, I will let you in."

The man stopped thumping on the door and glared up at Mir Alam.

"Don't you soil my father's name by uttering it, old man," he shouted. "Who have you got hidden inside here? Shooting at us? Hanh?"

"Arrey baba, I have known Jayant Bhai for longer than you have, I have seen you in nothing but your waist chain in his arms, and you tell me not to take your father's name? What kind of behaviour is this, boy? And as for shooting-wooting, I don't know what you are talking about. I was sitting here quietly and heard the same noises you did. My heart is still jumping in my chest with the shock. Arrey, let me tell you . . ."

"Bas, bas," snarled Jayant Bhai's son. "Enough of your useless *bakwas*. Now will you open this door and let us in or do you want me to break it down." He turned to the crowd behind him and said, "These *katlu* bastards talk too much. Soon we will settle their hash for them and then we will see who talks when and where."

The crowd growled appreciatively.

Mir Alam peered down hoping to catch a glimpse of his tenant shopkeeper Tika Ram. He was a reasonable fellow and as far as Mir Alam knew, they had no quarrel with each other. Ah there he was, at the back of the crowd. Mir Alam raised his hand to wave to him, but the shopkeeper did not respond. With a sigh, the old man turned and headed downstairs to open the front door. Better to do whatever they wanted and avoid trouble. These youngsters had no patience or respect any more.

Mir Alam was almost at the door when Edith decided to let off the last of her crackers. She had tottered back into the house after the first set of explosions, giggling at the sight of the panic-stricken pigeons. That would teach the wretched things to mess up her bedspread, she chuckled. That would teach Mir to laugh at her! She stooped to slip on her sandals before going across the landing for lunch, when she spotted the last string of red crackers draped across the arm of a chair where she had dropped it. Edith grinned to herself. Hah, one more good scare and those pigeons would never dare to come back here. She held the lighted candle to the long white string dangling from the bottom of the cracker and flung it with all her strength towards the balcony. It flew over the railings and exploded in a shower of sparks and bangs over the crowd.

There was a sudden stillness as before a thunderstorm and then the crowd erupted with rage. Mir Alam opened the front door with a smile on his face. He hadn't heard the last set of crackers go off, for age had stolen some of his hearing along with his eyesight.

"Come, come," he said, stepping out into the open. "Come and see whatever you want to, *beta*."

A stone sailed over his head and landed with a crash against a mirror in the dark corridor behind him. Mir Alam stopped smiling. Faster than he could think, a second and larger stone hit him on the face shattering his spectacles. A shard of glass pierced his eye and he fell to his knees in agony. Led by Jayant Bhai's son, the crowd surged into the house, their feet kicking at Mir Alam as he crouched by the door. He could hear the tinkle of broken glass, the dull thud of sticks battering down pictures and furniture, the muted roar of raging hearts. Above the stench of hate, he could smell Roshan's biryani. Any minute now Edith would be coming down in her yellow silk dress. Mir Alam rocked with pain as the piece of glass embedded in his eye worked its way in deeper every time he fluttered his lids. He tried to cling to rational thought, to the familiar. I will enclose Edith's balcony with chicken wire, he thought. That way she will not be disturbed by my darling pigeons and we will all be happy. I shouldn't have been so rude to her, poor lady, who else does she have in this foreign land but us? From the inside of his violated home he heard a long scream. Roshan, he thought dully, the pain of his eye clamouring against the nerve ends in his brain, what have they done to her? Mir Alam willed his tired old body to rise from the ground.

Outside the house, in the blue sky of a Sunday morning, a hundred pigeons wheeled and fluttered.

The Icicle

UMA PARAMESWARAN

The safety scanner light on the back door went on, filling the yard with light. Marzi, the neighbour's cat had been the cause; she lazily rubbed herself against the caragana bush and walked away. The light shone on the icicle hanging outside the window, and diamonds flashed for a few moments through the white cloud of the dryer exhaust which was just below the window. Then the light switched itself off.

I remembered something I had forgotten to do all week—to phone Ranjit to ask if I could borrow his tripod for the weekend. I had this toy that Sivaram had given me for New Year's, a camcorder, and I was going to take the most fantastic clips during the next few weeks, like the diamonds glistening off the icicle. I also had to write stories on video for my grandchildren, stories that my children had been asking me for years and that I had never got around to doing. What did it matter if the grandchildren were not born yet? One of these days they will arrive. As one of my tennis friends said, she had come to the point where she didn't care if her daughters never got married as long as they provided her with grandchildren.

Yes, I had to make video documentaries of how each of the stuffed toys we had adopted over the years had come home. Like Rakesh the raccoon, who had been sitting rather forlornly in a corner at a garage sale down the lane until I had swept him into my arms and brought him home, given him a lysol bath, and surgically replaced his tail.

The camcorder was state of the art; everything Sivaram buys is state of the art, he's one of those classy men who'd never ask the price of things, or god forbid go to a garage sale. I looked forward to using it but I had just figured out that the guys on television, who slung their state-of-the-art equipment easy as easy over their shoulders, were carnivores and so could probably lift twice their weight without so much as a heave. Salad-eating vegan that I am, I needed a tripod.

Maybe Ranjit had already left for Saskatoon, as he did every weekend since Deepa and little Anji had moved there. I phoned. He was still at home. Come on over, he said, I just came in, got a little late getting back from work, not starting for Saskatoon till tomorrow, so come on over.

It took me half an hour to clear the table, stack the dirty dishes in the dishwasher, hang out the shirts from the clothes-dryer etc. I got into my coat. Hnhn, Sivaram grunted, as I said bye bye. The six o'clock news was still on and so he probably had not registered what I'd said. That's what "hnhn" meant. "Okay!" meant my comment had been entered and his mind would process it later. "Drive carefully" meant he had really heard and registered at the same time, especially that I was taking his Volvo. Ranjit lived less than a mile away, and so the car had hardly got warm when I was at his door. Don't believe everything the salesmen and other owners say about a Volvo. We've always had a Volvo, but that's another story.

Ranjit opened the door. Come on in, he said, I just have to turn off my computer.

What are you surfing? I asked, pretending to know all the right jargon. Just reading the chess column, he said, did you hear about how Kasparov got beaten by a computer?

In one corner were stacked a couple of cartons and a child's desk and a huge stuffed toy, a panda. This one was white with black eyes the way pandas are supposed to be, unlike our Rakesh, who was blue and had white-rimmed black eyes and a black-ringed blue tail. So we'd never figured out whether he was a panda or a raccoon.

I moved some newspapers from the sofa to the table so I could sit. The couch had a couple of pillows and the recliner a blanket. Both couch and recliner were angled just right for the screen of the television set, which was on the sports channel. I figured, from the plates and potato chips and beer mug on the side tables, that Ranjit lived in the living room whenever he was home, moving from recliner to couch when he wanted a change. The house had a musty winter smell, of cooking spices and cigarette smoke and beer, that had piled up in the closed rooms. In a few minutes, as always with such smells, I got used to it.

Can I get you a cup of coffee? he said, bringing the tripod to the living room.

So tell me all the news, he said.

Not a one, I said.

Come on, Maru, so who has had a baby, who is getting married etc. etc. Or tell me about your volunteer work; how is the old cow, your boss?

Don't be such a gossip, Ranjit. How are you doing?

Till Deepa moved, I had my line to community happenings; now I am totally out of everything. Just me and my work, waiting for the weekend.

You haven't missed even one weekend, eh? I said admiringly.

Not me, Maru. Anji will never be four again. I just can't miss out on this. It is so incredibly precious. Each week it seems like she's grown. And she can't wait to tell me what she has learnt at daycare. I am so glad we got her into the University daycare. She loves it. And Deepa can study without worrying, that's a great help.

But isn't it tiring for you driving all the way Friday and Sunday evenings?

No sweat, just a straight road that you can drive on with eyes closed. Oh, you should see the way she throws herself onto our bed Saturday morning. We let Mom sleep in while we take off. Did you know she's started adding? I took her an abacus a few weeks ago, and now you should see her! She is so much into drawing too. I am taking her this desk, see the way it opens up like a little easel, get it? Marty made it for his kids, and now it's mine. Hohoho. Being a parent is like being Santa Claus all year round. Shit, I miss not having her here.

No denying you are Santa, I said. The basement is so chock full of toys. You really should think of donating the playpen and stroller and car seat and whatnot before they get mildewed down there.

He put his hands behind his back and looked out the window. Would be nice to have another kid, he said. Not good to be an only child. He turned and looked at me. I worry, Maru, I do. Life is so unpredictable. Who knows how long we'd be around to take care of her? I mean, she needs people, family. Like, I just lift up the receiver and talk to my brother in Jaipur.

When did you call him last? I laughed.

That's not the point. I know my brother and sisters are there for me, no matter where we are . . . I'd like to buy a safe car, you know what I mean? I worry . . . our other car is a jalopy, much worse than the one I have here . . . It is just for within the city, Deepa says and shrugs it off. But did you know that most accidents take place within ten kilometres of home? Every weekend I think I'll leave my car there but let's face it, I can't afford to take risks—a couple of weekends ago, there was this behemoth of an accident just ahead of me—not until Anji is a little older at least, and Deepa lands a job maybe.

Ranjit, you are turning into a worry wart. Come to think of it, you've always been one. So how's your new job?

No big deal. Same paper-shuffling and boring programming, but at least I don't have to be on the road all the time and work up sales. Less money but this one leaves me free weekends. And that's worth everything else put together. Anji will never be four again, Maru. Oh you've got to come with me some weekend and see for yourself.

I'd love to see her, I said. No chance of them coming over some long weekend? It is months since they were here.

Oh I don't know. Deepa is always rather busy. These courses with practicals keep students hopping. She's also working with some Nursing Home where her prof has a project going. She's doing very well, though. Straight A's all the way.

I could hear the pride in his voice. I remembered, too, his frustration three years ago when Deepa was looking for work. It burns me up Maru, he had said, to see her working in Henry Armstrong's Instant Printing for god's sake; I mean she is a straight A student and they are telling her her Delhi degrees don't count, and so she ends up replacing toners in bloody duplicating machines. Sometimes I think I should run for the legislature and get some action going, really. Pisses me off, all this racism. Say, did I show you her grad pics from last Fall? I took them with this tripod and my Canon.

Yes, Ranj, you did, about a dozen times if you want to know, though

I'd be delighted to look at them, all fifty of them, over again if you could find the album under all this rubble.

He moved his hands in a one-two punch at me. Aye Maru, he said, you're a one.

I took out the pop-up picture book I had brought for Anji. From what you say, I said, may be she's outgrown this already.

He smiled proudly. She's my daughter, never forget that, Maru. Say, have I told you how her name is just so right, though I never realized it when I insisted on naming her that?

Anjali? an offering as in Tagore's *Gitanjali*? I remembered him reciting Tagore soon after her birth.

Yeah that too. But I mean Anji as in inside Ranjit? got it? He placed his hand on his heart. Shit, why is it only women get to carry the tykes inside?

I'd better be going, I said, it has started snowing already. They are forecasting heavy snow for tomorrow.

Oh shit, really? He took up the remote control and switched to the weather channel. Oh shit, I thought of leaving early morning. I guess I'd better get started right away and beat the blizzard. Oh shit. Sorry to boot you out, Maru, thanks for dropping by.

I should be thanking you, I said.

Any time, Maru, any time. You can keep the tripod till the cows come home. All my gear is out in Saskatoon, and by now I've got it all figured out how to sit my camcorder on my shoulder.

You have? Tell me the secret.

He smiled. Uh unh. Okay, seeing as you are my best friend and all, you can get it at any photo place. Don's, Astral, Japan Camera.

He put on his coat and took up his overnight satchel. He picked up the panda from the sofa. I guess the other things will have to wait till next Friday. So what do you think your name is going to be? he said, giving the panda a squeeze.

Panduranga, I said, tell Anji his name is Panduranga the panda. But wait, what do I ask for? a shoulder strap?

I love your ignorance, Maru, love you. He smiled. He had a charming smile, a little boy's smile, his eyes dancing with light. It made my heart ache to see that smile, and my eyes wandered to the bookshelf where within a diamond-studded glass frame he and Anji flanked Deepa in her baccalaureate convocation gown. I went up to him and gave him a hug. Drive carefully, little brother, I said, using the diminutive of my own Tamil language which could better express the gut-wrenching affection and sadness I felt for him. Drive carefully, little brother, and give my love to Deepa and Anji.

We walked out of the house together, he to his battered Toyota, I to Sivaram's new Volvo. Can't he see, I cried to myself, the whole convocation album scrolling on my mental screen, he so happy and proud and hugging her in every one of them, and she drawing away from his touch. It was only a matter of time.

*

"First name in fashion designs, sixth letter 'i'," Sivaram said, his pencil poised over the morning crossword. "And Michael Jackson's famous gait, take a break, who can remember such old hat?"

"Moonwalk," I said. "You always get the answer to clues like 'Scarlett's locale' or 'one of the musketeers.'"

"Those are classics. There's a difference, in case you haven't thought about it. I can wager even kids now fifteen wouldn't know Michael Jackson from a hole in the wall. By the way, I have to go to Saskatoon first weekend of next month."

"Great," I said. "I'll come along."

He lowered his head and looked at me from above his reading glasses. "Saskatoon, not Sweden or Sasquatch. You want to come to Saskatoon? As in Regina-Saskatoon?"

"Yes, sure do. Meet some old friends. Like Deepa. She called me just yesterday, and today you tell me you have a meeting in Saskatoon. Don't you think there's something to the coincidence?"

"Like divine providence leading you?"

I shrugged, "Why not?" There was no need to tell him that Deepa called me routinely once every few weeks.

"Is she still out there? Maybe that explains it. I ran into Ranjit the other day and he looked out of sorts. Or maybe he's lost some hair or weight or something. He looked different. Are they still together?"

"Of course they are together."

"Okay okay, don't blow a fuse. Your feminist crowd break up all the time, even lesbians, I mean. So what is Deepa doing? Physiotherapy, is it?"

"She is working on her Master's," I said. "Doing very well, too. She hopes to get an assistantship soon."

"You mean you're going to let her join the slave pack?" He smiled.

That had been one of our frequent points of dissension. In recent years, he had taken to bringing over graduate students from India, and paying them peanuts. I felt he was exploiting them. He maintained that he was doing them a favour. Did I know of the recent changes in Immigration policy? That if one wasn't related to someone already here or wasn't an entrepreneur with a million dollars, there was absolutely no way one could get into the country? Six percent was all they admitted in the Independent category, did I know that? In our days, if we had brains, we could come and help both ourselves and the country get ahead. I mean what future was there for Canada if we only allowed six percent as independents? So our people, he still said "our people" even though he had spent more of his life outside India than in, could come in only as students. Not with a job or even as post-docs as most of us did. No not even for a PhD because of course no one had grants to support them. Only as grad students in the Master's programme; so he chose these bright young men from middle-class families and gave them a foothold into the country. (And peanuts, I said.) So what if they lived for a year or two in basement rooms along Silverstone and Townsend, and on peanuts and snow? And take my word, Canada will be the richer for them, which is more than I can say of my Canadian-born undergraduates, even those with parents born elsewhere. (If they didn't run off to the States, I said.) If Immigration would admit more graduate students instead of reintegrating so-called families and having to monitor and/or encourage marriages of convenience by opportunists . . . The argument always ended in a tie. "Ranjit is supporting her all the way, of course, but an assistantship would help," I said, remembering what Ranjit had told me about wanting a safe car.

"Would you please phone me around eleven today so I can get Beth to book your ticket along with mine? And whether you'll be staying with me or with Deepa. Unless, of course, you think I shouldn't ask Beth."

That was another of our bones of contention—the way bosses asked their secretaries to make the coffee and do their personal work.

"I'll stay with you Thursday for sure," I said. "The first evening is always fun at your conferences. Giorgio," I said, "Giorgio Armani. And isn't Sasquatch a yeti or something?"

"Thanks," he said. "Didn't think you'd notice. Just assume I said Surabaya or Swaziland." And went on to solve the day's cryptogram.

*

Deepa came to our hotel at nine that Friday morning to pick me up. The first thing that hit me was that she was looking beautiful. A kind of glow that can come only from within. I hadn't seen her like that since the time Anji was about due. While Ranjit hovered and worried himself sick over her, she just sat smiling, with that glow on and around her, as though she knew everything about her birthing would be, could not but be, perfectly normal.

How happy they had been then, those last few months and the first few months. Ranj did everything around the house, cooked and cleaned, and washed the dirty diapers—no rash-prone non-eco-conscious disposables or diaper service for his baby, nothing but cotton diapers laundered at home and aired in the sun. Did I know the Vitamin A in the sun was good even for clothes?

"It's going to work out so well," Deepa said, "that you've come on a Friday. I am taking the day off and Anji will be at daycare till four and that will leave us the time to catch up on all the news."

"You are looking gorgeous," I said, getting into her car. "Looks like you like what you are doing."

"Oh yes yes yes," she said, "every minute of it."

She told me about her work, her classes, her professor's project. Massage therapy, meditation, holistic care. He was trying to tabulate and formulate, see why the body reacted the way it did, and please don't tell me people in India and China knew all about it centuries ago. She was more interested in the actual results. To see a wasted limb get back to being functional . . . it was so tangible, so real, so worthwhile. I was being carried into her high.

We went to her department, where she had a few chores to finish. I sat in her cubicle and flipped through some journals while she did her work. The cubicle was piled high with library books—on the table, the shelves, the floor. Only the computer desk in the corner was neat and functional. Beside it was stacked the first draft of the first chapter of her thesis. It was creditable how far she had come and how fast. It was less than a year since she had started her Master's programme. I felt proud of her, my protégé.

The years of her bachelor's programme had been rough, not because of her skills or time, but because she knew the crossroads that awaited her once she had her degree. She had delayed completing her programme, while she endlessly debated with herself as to what she should do. I was the only one privy to her debates. She would talk and talk. Just my being there so she could debate aloud helped her get the courage to take her decision. She knew very well what she wanted to do but she needed the time to process it through her psychological channels, to arrive at a point where she could live with herself for taking the decision.

Now I sat back and listened to the sound of her voice as she discussed something with a colleague in another cubicle. Technical jargon flowed back and forth, and there was so much confidence in her tone as she debated the issue. I didn't listen to what was being said, but I was filled with delight at how happy she sounded, and when she laughed, it was so carefree, like she was home free.

We went to her apartment. It was just four blocks from the University, and overlooked a playground. "I have been so lucky all the way," Deepa said, "Anji just loves to stand on the sofa and watch the playground while I get dinner ready. Not that I cook much; Anji has a good breakfast; she is addicted to her cheese sandwich for lunch, and milk and apple when she comes home. But dinner has to be coaxed in, spoon by spoon. Thank god she eats vegetables and all that at least during the weekends."

"So when are you coming to Winnipeg?" I said at some point. "You used to come often enough but you haven't been there for, how long?"

"I am not counting," she said, "the longer the better. Those weekends used to wipe me out. I ended up cooking and cleaning all day every day, feeding all the people who had invited him over in my absence; I had to slog to pay back for what he had enjoyed. Ugh. And the house was always such a mess. Knowing I would come, he never lifted a finger between my visits. Not that he helped in any way when I was there, for that matter. He has been a couch potato ever since I went back to University. I had to earn my tuition fees, that is the way he saw it, I guess. Wonder what he does now. Gets a cleaning woman, I suppose."

I was not ready to answer. But she did not seem to expect or want one. She went on to talk about Anji.

"She must love having him here every weekend," I said.

"Why wouldn't she," she said. "He spoils her rotten."

"Children can be spoilt but there's no such thing as being spoilt rotten," I said. "Love is one commodity that never stales."

"I can handle love," she said. "Anything that doesn't occupy space or can be eaten up. But he brings her things every weekend. Just look around you, Maru," she said. "Soon we won't have any room to move. See that desk? He brought it a few weeks ago, it is supposed to be an easel for his daughter's masterpieces. Really. And the stuffed toys! You won't believe the size of the panda he brought the time we had that storm, I don't know if you had it out there. And father and kid give names to each of these stuffed animals. It takes Anji half an hour every day to say goodnight to her toys. Really, he spoils her rotten and it takes me two days to get her back on track, and two days later he's here again. UND has a better programme, you know, but I figured Grand Forks, and even Fargo were too close and that the eight hour drive to Saskatoon would faze him and so I chose this place. Boy, was I wrong! I sure am looking forward to the day when I can go farther than driving distance and have Anji all to myself."

"But he loves her," I said. "It would break his heart."

"Oh, how I wish he'd just find some other woman and get out of my hair," she said.

The Spaces Between Stars

GEETA KOTHARI

Watching the fish squirm in Evan's gloved hands, Maya was transfixed by the fish's suffering. It had stopped moving for a second, but now it was struggling, its tail flapping back and forth, as it twisted for freedom, unaware that the hook lodged deep in its gut wouldn't let go.

"It's dying," she said. "We should have pushed down the barbs like that woman in the store told us to."

Evan grunted and peered inside the fish's mouth.

"I know what I'm doing."

Maya knew he was determined to give her a genuine, all-American fishing trip, the kind he used to go on when he was a boy outdoors, and she was a girl indoors, watching TV. Long before Evan, there had been a boy on TV, a boy with long lanky hair that hung across one eye. He had flicked it back impatiently as he baited his hook, explaining to the camera that the "crick" was his favourite place. She remembered that word "crick" because some of the kids at school said it, kids who were unaware of her but whom she observed from a distance.

The small sunfish, a swath of green and gold, glistened in Evan's hand. The sun beat down on the top of Maya's head, searing her scalp. She felt dizzy and a wave of sadness passed over her as she stared at the helpless fish.

"It's dying."

Evan gently placed the sunfish in the water and cut the line. It swam off, seemingly recovered from its near-death experience.

To cook the fish he had caught, the boy on TV dug up some fresh clay, patted it into two flat rounds, stuck the fish between them and baked it in the flames of his campfire. In her dreams, Maya would camp by that "crick," fish and swim in it and sleep in a tent under the stars. How she would see the stars above her head while sleeping in a tent, she wasn't sure, but even in her fantasy life, she could not see herself sleeping without shelter.

Maya climbed back into the boat. Her line had been cut, and her mission had been achieved. She proved herself able to catch a fish, and now she wanted to go home. She handed Evan a turkey sandwich and looked over the side of the boat. Her fish, red at the gills, eyes bulging, floated towards them.

"Look," she said. "It died anyway."

Evan shrugged. "It was just a sunfish. They're everywhere."

Her guilt pressed against her temples, tightening like vice around her head. Still she said nothing. She'd been the one who not only agreed but had been excited about going fishing. It had been one of the many activities forbidden to her during childhood. The expedition should have made her feel closer to Evan. Instead, Maya felt as if the parched brown hills surrounding the lake had sprung up between them. The inside of her skin itched, and she wanted to jump out of it, leave behind her body and the pervasive smell of dead fish.

She watched Evan eat his sandwich, oblivious to her inner turmoil as he basked in the sun. He was like that boy on TV. He was resourceful, knew how to do things that were beyond her realm of experience. He could pitch a tent, start a campfire, handle raw meat without feeling sick, open the hood of a car and see things. He could talk to strangers and get his way. Evan assumed he had the right number until told otherwise; he assumed cooperation and satisfaction, even when talking to the phone company about a bill. Making calls from one of her temporary jobs, Maya would begin her sentences with "I'm not sure . . ." and end them breathless, gasping for air, as she struggled to find the right words. Eventually, passed from one person to the next, trying to make herself understood, she would give up and leave the task for the next day. What looked like procrastination was something she couldn't begin to explain.

She had wanted to be that boy on TV, but what such boys were seemed hereditary, increasingly out of reach and unattainable. Instead, she forced herself through college and one dismal semester of graduate school. And then she married Evan.

*

They got home late in the afternoon, just as the thunder started rolling in. Evan shut himself up in his study while Maya napped. The heat, the death of the fish, had exhausted her leaving her empty and dry inside.

Later, she made dinner, though she had no appetite or enthusiasm for the aloo gobi and dal. Nothing smelled or tasted right; the potatoes and cauliflower were mushy and the dal was limp and tasteless. Her shoulders felt sore from the sun, and the smell of blood lingered on her fingers. She felt dirty, stained by the death of the sunfish. She rubbed her fingers with lemon juice until her cuticles burned, and still they smelled.

Evan padded into the kitchen, his blond hair sticking up as if he'd been sleeping and pulled a beer out of the refrigerator.

"Indian food. What's the occasion?" He leaned against the counter and stretched his legs across the narrow passage. Everything about him was long, lean and graceful. Next to him, she felt like a clumsy baby elephant—small, dark, and always in his shadow.

"None. Should there be?"

"You never make it, that's all."

"That's because I can't." Her voice got tighter, and she felt a rush of anger, making her face hotter above the steaming pots.

But Evan would not be drawn into a fight. "Don't forget, my folks are coming next week. And they want an answer about the trip."

Maya's stomach dropped. She'd forgotten both the ski trip at Christmas and the Everetts' impending visit.

Fortunately, the Everetts would stay with friends, as they always did. Though they'd never said anything, Maya sensed that she didn't keep house up to their standards. The brass incense holder, the small footstool inlaid with ivory, the embroidered mirror-work cushions, and the orange and red batik wall hangings had been passed on to her by her aunt, Shyamma. They seemed to go well with the reupholstered couch and chair from Evan's parents, but she was sure they didn't find the same comfort in this mixed decor.

Maya checked the cumin-flavoured rice. When she looked up, she noticed that Evan was still in the room, watching her as she moved from stove to sink, counter to kitchen table. "Are you all right?" he asked.

"Fine." He was the psychologist, she thought. Let him figure it out.

"Really?" He came over and kissed the back of her neck while she fluffed the rice. The individual grains had lost their definition and clung together, exactly what the recipe warned against.

"Allergies," she said, shrugging him off. Her long dark hair was coming out of its elastic band, sticking to the back of her sweaty neck. His lips against her skin reminded her of the fish, gasping for breath.

She couldn't tell him. She couldn't admit her failure of will, of heart, in the great American outdoors. It was simply beyond her, to find the words for this thing she couldn't understand.

After dinner, Shyamma called.

First, she complained about the weather.

"Yesterday, I forgot to drink even one glass of water. Can you imagine? I nearly fainted in the kitchen."

"You have to pay attention, auntie." Maya could not call her Shyamma, the way Evan did, not out loud, even though Shyamma had told her to. "The heat isn't your friend, just because you don't like the cold."

Three, four times a week, Shyamma would call with a muted crisis or a question that needed an immediate response. A response, not an answer, Maya finally understood, and she listened, for Shyamma was the only family she had.

"And how is that husband of yours?"

"Fine. He's nearly finished." Evan was working on his dissertation, and it gave Shyamma great pleasure to finally have a PhD in the family. Evan's success made up nicely for the brilliant failure of Maya's academic career.

Maya wondered what Shyamma would say about her aborted conversion into a fisherwoman and her complicity in the death of the sunfish. What was okay for an Everett might be unacceptable for a Sohni. Shyamma was still a vegetarian. She prayed to her blue-faced gods and goddesses, and every day at sunset, burnt sweetgrass and sage on a small piece of charcoal, carrying it reverently from room to room in the small house Maya had grown up in.

Shyamma asked about the Everetts, their two daughters, and everyone else under the Everett sun.

"Such a nice family." She sighed.

"Because they invite you to their stupid Christmas party?" Maya chewed a hangnail, enjoying the sharp pain that ran through her finger.

"Yes. And they always send me cards—Halloween, Easter, Christmas."

Holidays Shyamma used to dismiss as "Christian" or "American," having nothing to do with them. Not even a Christmas tree, Maya thought, and now she eats cookies shaped like Santa Claus and sings "Away in the Manger" without hesitation. After five years, she knew the words by heart, just like everyone else at the party.

"And so," Shyamma finally said. "How are you?"

"Fine. We went fishing today."

"That's nice bacchi." Maya listened to the pots and pan clattering in the background. She doubted her aunt had heard her. Their conversation was over.

*

Shyamma had raised Maya alone, after her parents were killed in a plane crash. Rather than send Maya back to live with her paternal grandparents, Shyamma insisted on keeping her in the States. She herself didn't want to go back to India and marry the demented distant cousin her father had found for her.

"Understand," Shyamma once said, "I had a fellowship, and I was finally free. And I was afraid if I sent you to your father's people, we'd never see you."

They had been lonely in Erie. They knew no other Indian families with children. Most of Shyamma's friends were single women who worked full-time. She seemed not to miss her family whom they saw on rare visits to Delhi. Now, though, her loneliness had caught up with her. Maya heard it in the phone calls, the unasked "When are you next coming up?" During those cold, dreary winters, when the wind blew hard off the lake and kept them inside, Shyamma would tell Maya what a great life they had, how easy it was to be American, how good this country had been to her. But for Maya, growing up in a strict vegetarian household in Erie during the sixties was not fun. Her aunt, Shyamma, banned Oreos because they were made with lard. At barbecues and school picnics, Maya hid her plate, heavy with potato salad, corn on the cob, coleslaw and an empty hot dog bun. Shyamma saw to it that Maya ate nutritionally sound meals, overlooking the conflict between this and Maya's sole desire: to be like everyone else and not like her aunt, who still lived in the culture she'd left over thirty years ago.

On their last trip to Erie, Maya and Evan had found Shyamma chilled and sick with the flu. She had hid it from them, she said, because she was afraid they wouldn't come up. The walk at Presque Isle, promised to Evan, was put off; it was too cold, even if they were healthy, Shyamma insisted. They spent the whole weekend indoors. Evan paced the small living room and stared out the window the way Maya used to when she was a child. Shyamma lay on the couch, reading magazines and marking all the things she would someday buy, when she had enough money. Her salary from the hospital was never quite enough; she was a woman with foreign syntax and got paid less than any man in the same position.

Such was Shyamma's freedom.

*

Later, in bed, Evan asked Maya again about the ski trip. His parents wanted to take them to Banff at Christmas, where a friend of theirs would let them stay for free.

"I don't think so."

Evan sat up and looked at her. Maya kept her eyes focussed on her book and remained slouched against the headboard.

"You always said you wanted—"

"I'm too old. Why don't you go without me?"

Evan ran his hand through his hair. He looked at her for a minute and then got out of bed.

"Fine. You figure out a way to tell my parents why you're not coming."

Evan, Maya had learned a long time ago, was uninterested in confrontation, in talking things through. He left the room and she heard him go into his study. He would work for the next few hours, slip into bed after she'd fallen asleep, and dream through the conflict. The next morning, he'd act as if nothing had been said, and by evening he'd be asking her the same question again. And if she did not give him the answer he wanted, the whole scene would repeat itself, day after day, until one of them—usually Maya—gave in.

*

She woke up early the next morning. Next to her, Evan slept soundly. Maya pushed his thin hair off his face and traced the outline of his ear, half willing him to wake up. He turned over to his other side, pulling the sheet with him. When she slid out of bed, he didn't move.

Down in the kitchen, watching the sky get lighter over the river, she smelled it, the dead fish smell. She sniffed the carton of cream, her fingers, the tail of her long braid. She opened the refrigerator, scanning the shelves for any forgotten beans, unwrapped meat or cheese. She pulled open the vegetable bin, checking for wilted broccoli, mushy tomatoes, and soggy lettuce. She threw out some mouldy cottage cheese and a dried-up piece of fudge cake.

Maya's feet stuck to the kitchen floor as she scrubbed the cabinet doors.

"You are so ungrateful," Shyamma used to say, when Maya was sixteen and came home at two in the morning, smelling of alcohol and back seat sex.

Maya shrugged. It didn't matter what she did, Shyamma would be there. They were family, blood in a world of strangers. Like fish, they swam in the same school, a school of two, but a school nonetheless, dodging predators, careful of false bait.

Maya had finally bitten. Life with Evan was too tempting, an easy guarantee that she would not end up like Shyamma. But the ski trip weighed on her, pulling her in a direction she wasn't sure she wanted to go. Evan's parents had welcomed her as easily as they welcomed Shyamma; now she wished for a little resistance—a disapproving arched eyebrow or a look of confusion when they saw her living room, would have been good. Instead, Pat had smiled into the tiny mirrors, and Evy nodded as he eased himself in his old chair. She and Shyamma had done everything to make themselves acceptable, so why should the mixed decor worry the Everetts?

Maya brushed her teeth until her gums bled and the brush hurt her cheek. Once on a bus she saw a man scratching his arms with a steel pick comb, running it up and down along his forearm, until the skin was raised in thin red welts that looked ready to burst.

"Heroin addict," Shyamma said, after the man stumbled off the bus.

"How do you know?"

"When they need a fix, they itch so bad, they want to jump out of their skin. That was him."

Looking at her reflection in the bathroom mirror, Maya felt the same way. She wanted out of this skin, out of this life and into another, one that fit her, not one that she had to fit.

*

That night, when Evan asked again, Maya said, "I don't want to go."

She lay in bed, flat on her back. Light from the house next door cut through the open blinds, striping the rumpled cotton sheets. She stared at the ceiling, searching for the fluorescent stars Evan had pasted on it when they first moved in.

Evan rolled over on his side, facing her. "If it's the money—"

"It's not the money."

"Then what is it?"

Maya flopped over, turning her back to him. "When I was a kid, all I ever wanted was to go on our school ski trips. Every year they had one, and all the cool people went. Those who couldn't afford it did cross-country on their own. Shyamma wouldn't even let me do that. When I said she didn't trust me to take care of myself, she said it was the cold too cold for me. She really meant it was too cold for her."

"So here's your chance," Evan said.

"I don't care anymore. I can't do it."

"You won't even try."

She turned to face him. In the dark, she couldn't read his expression, but she resisted the urge to turn the light on.

"Why is it so important that I ski?"

Evan sighed. "You're part of the family."

"Ralph doesn't ski. He's still part of the family, isn't he?" Evan's older brother-in-law refused to put on skis for political and economic reasons that the entire family teased him about.

"He's just scared."

"So? I bet Anne isn't forcing him to go to Banff."

"Jesus." Evan punched his pillow. "You're the one who wanted to go fishing, you wanted to ski, and now you're blaming me." He left the room, slamming the door behind him, and then slamming his study door as well.

Maybe she was scared. What if she couldn't really be an Everett? She was still horrified by her participation in the death of another creature. It was all very well to kill a fish on television or buy it at the store, nicely cleaned and filleted, but this—this was the beginning of a cycle she'd never be able to escape.

But what was the alternative? Maya lay on her back. On the ceiling, the stars glowed. There was the Big Dipper, the Little Dipper, Orion, the archer. Evan had followed the instructions so precisely, the whole sky filled their ceiling. When she initially suggested it, she'd thought of scattering them where she pleased. While she was out one day, Evan put them up, arranging each and every one just so.

When she showed her surprise, he frowned and said, "But that's how they're supposed to be. Every star in its place."

And where was hers? She had thought with Evan she would find it. But only if she forgot where she'd been before, and now she found that forgetting incomplete.

*

The next morning, Maya woke up at dawn and was on the road before the sun had completely risen. She didn't want to give herself the chance to change her mind and seeing Evan would have done that. She drove north on 79, past Mars, Moon Township, and the shrine in the median at Zelienople. A marker for someone who had died on the road, the small fir tree was decorated for July 4—red, white, and blue tinsel draped over it and an American flag languidly moving in the slipstream of the big trucks that roared by. At Easter, pastel-coloured plastic eggs hung from its branches, and at Christmas someone garnished it with bright ornaments, including a gold angel for the top. She'd seen similar shrines on the Mass Pike and the New Jersey Turnpike, so unusual they'd caught her eye.

By the time she pulled into Shyamma's neat little driveway, with the marigolds lined up on either side, it was well past eight o'clock. She knew that Shyamma would be in the kitchen. Maybe she could talk her into making some masala chai, something to wash her mouth of the terrible McDonald's coffee she'd had an hour ago.

Shyamma didn't look up from the counter where she was rolling out some dough.

"Evan called. He wants to know if you'll be home for dinner."

Her tone was accusing, on Evan's behalf.

"I left him a note."

Shyamma tucked a strand of hair behind her ear. Her hair was still black and shiny, a testament to the coconut oil she used regularly and rigorous brushing. Her small brown face was slack at the jaw and under the chin, but her cheeks were high and firm, turning into small apples when she smiled. She had a sweet smile, Evan said, like Maya. But neither of them was smiling now.

"Paratha?"

"Stuffed kulcha." Shyamma kept rolling the small rounds of springy dough.

"For breakfast?" Maya was used to seeing the stuffed bread on special occasions only.

"No one here to tell me I can't."

She put the water to boil, in a saucepan, Maya noticed with relief. If Shyamma was making masala chai, Maya was not in that much trouble.

"I killed a fish." The words sounded terrible out loud, damning, yet she understood in that moment why criminals often confessed. A fleeting lightness lifted in her as she waited for her aunt's absolution.

'Did you eat it?"

"No." What did her aunt think she was? "I tried to save its life."

Shyamma added two teaspoons of tea to the boiling water and some milk. She let it boil vigorously, like the chai-wallahs back home did, in huge pots on single burners.

"Sounds like a contradiction."

"It was an accident."

They ate in silence, at the same formica-topped table Shyamma had bought twenty years ago at a yard sale. The kulcha was slightly burnt, crispy at the edges and soft in the middle. Maya couldn't remember when it had tasted so good. "You don't have to come here every time you want a stuffed kulcha."

Shyamma cleared the dishes as she spoke. Maya had the impression she was going somewhere, that she didn't want her to stay.

"I know." She had the recipe, carefully pasted into a notebook with a number of other recipes Shyamma had insisted on showing her. At the time, she'd resisted; it seemed unnecessary, going back to a time when girls were prepared for marriage. Now she understood Shyamma had not been preparing her for anyone but herself.

As it turned out, Shyamma did have plans. She was going to a friend's house to discuss their Christmas vacation, a cruise somewhere warm and tropical. Maya hid her surprise; the only holidays her aunt had ever taken were their trips to India. Not wanting to even slightly dissuade her, Maya said nothing. She took the leftover kulcha and headed home, with promises to bring Evan back in a few weeks.

When she got home, Evan was out. She went straight to the bedroom and dug around for the leftover stars stashed in her bedside table. She cleared off the table and stood on it; using the wall for balance, she added her own star to the cluster directly above her side of the bed.

All these years, she thought the answer lay in teaching Shyamma to love the cold. Maybe she was wrong.

*

Maya sat on the porch staring across the river. The sun had nearly set and the air felt like rain, heavy and full of promise. Her skin was clammy from the heat and humidity, but it didn't bother her. It reminded her of the way she felt in the monsoon, just before the rains came, turning the streets into muddy rivers that came up to her knees.

The door opened, and she saw Evan's shadow cast down the stairs. He stood for a moment in the doorway, drinking a beer.

"Nice night," he said.

His voice was low and cautious as he sat down next to her. Maya couldn't bring herself to look at his face, that sweet combination of dimples and blue eyes that showed his confusion no matter how hard he tried to hide it. Instead, she looked at his feet, grimy from a barefoot summer, the toenails ridged and hard, dirt rimming the cuticles. Later, maybe, his nails would scratch dully against her legs, her ankles, and the tops of her feet, leaving white lines and marks across her own dry brown skin, never hard enough to draw blood, but enough to mark Evan on her.

"Shyamma used to have a small shrine in the corner of our kitchen." Her voice was hoarse from thirst and silence. "Incense, flowers, an old calendar painting of Ganesh. That's all. Whenever I had friends over, I'd try to keep them from going in there."

"Why?"

"So I wouldn't have to hear them laugh and say, 'Ew, what's that?' and then explain why my aunt was worshipping a god with an elephant head."

"The god of all beginnings and the remover of obstacles." Evan sat down next to her.

"Shyamma told you that."

"When we got married."

Maya smiled. At the time, she would have forbidden the mention of Ganesh or any other god at her wedding, yet Shyamma had managed to find a space for him.

"I'm going to the temple when she comes."

One day, Shyamma will be gone, she thought, and I want to be left with more than the calendar image of a pot-bellied, elephant god.

He took her hand and squeezed it. "Want me to come?" "No. But no more fishing trips, okay?"

Maya drew a sip of beer from the long-necked bottle, letting a few drops drip down her chin. She held the cool glass against her temple and watched the lights come on across the river, solitary stars dotting a dark, lonely land. Evan put his hand on the back of her neck and stroked the damp hairs hanging out of her bun. They sat for a long time in silence, listening to the cicadas buzzing in the still heat, waiting for the storm to break and the sky to clear.

Hair

YASMIN LADHA

(i) rosy heat

Ancient Ayurvedic pastes and powders of *vaidans* and healers has gone Body Shop, filling Maa-earth in translucent reusables. The whiz idea of *au naturale* on skin in healing Maa-earth plastics, catapulted by that shaggy-haired folksy Brit, the she-guru of lotion-cum-environment. (Her husband is a poet I read in a weekend paper.)

Now the Indians have taken off (palming off really) on the folksy Brit's packaging, even her wide bottles with zippo sensuality of coffee flasks. But at least, beautiks and homeopathy aren't in tonic bottles of my childhood, anymore. Or dun powders in triangle pouches out of newspapers, which turn your sheets pee yellow when you sweat out the fetid rot in the night.

In the flushed boom-Indo-boom of the nineties, the commerce of vegetable heat and maroon juices and *vibuti* barks are packed in airy reusables (against animal testing, of course, just like the real B Shop). But even in Aryan-ancient of four thousand years ago, *Ayurveda* had a hoppy name—the green medicine shop. The skilled *vaidan* boiled herbs, spitty leaves, baby-hand vegetation from the skull of the Himalayas, petals bright as botched-up tongues, customized it all to a patient's ailment, then called the compound a decoration!

My environment-cum-bliss oil has *ambla*, centella, coconut, goat milk, cow milk, and *butea frondosa* (familiarly poetic like buttery Fabergé to me). I remember the advertisement not to pile your hair all on the top when you shampoo, or was it Pantene? My nineties coconut *butea frondosa* is in a green-capped bottle. And the king of my hair is the awesome BhringRaj. Though in the environmental age, he is now called Bio BhringRaj. I have known the King since my childhood, when I sat between my Grandmother's legs, my head lightly rocking back and forth as she oiled my hair. She swore by the King. In this age of cyber@environ, his name is majestic but teddy-bear snug too, like tech and bio putting up their feet in my kitchen without freaky beeps or avant garde composting. BhringRaj, the rajah of rajahs from my Grandmother's stories: chesty, jewelled, righteous, and celibate.

According to Grandmother, celibate rajahs are made of sterner stuff. They know focus and they know fixation. In other words, they brook no malarkey on the path of the straight and narrow. So naturally, my confidence in Rajah BhringRaj is gusty. He will pull and whack my scalp shafts into a thicket. Maharaj BhringRaj will whip a lush sheath well below my waist, slightly rosy with heat.

(ii) annals of hair

—tangled as beach salt
—a cashew swirl at the very nape
—an Audrey Hepburn pile-up
—lank as bare breasts
—a side-parted tumble
—brittle as stale roti
—coaxed the morning after
—plump with shine
—haughty as the second wife
—torn, unbound for fourteen rage years
—every ragged hair drinking the violator's gut
—and a woman pulls up a slow dazzling red bun

fourteen years dripping like stars, dripping from an avenger's dazzling bun. The avenger's name is Draupadi. On that humiliating day, her god, Krishna-the-blue, saves her. He stands behind her, invisible to others in the royal court, and slips yards and yards of spuming silk around her waist. The violator-prince (even in the cyber@environ.

times, it's usually a prince, sheikh, big-wig, or a king's soldier) tugs and tugs and the sari he has undone just makes silken dunes of mustard, peacock blue, turquoise, wet green, scarlet, corn yellow, warm maroon, and palatial purple on his court floor . . . but he can't strip her naked. From this day on, Draupadi leaves her hair unbound, waiting for the day when she can squish his gut, soak every sickle strand of her hair in it and pull up a slow dazzling red bun. Such stories dripped from Grandmother as she oiled my hair, thumped her palm all over my skull.

I would lift the foul bottle from the sill at the top of the kitchen door (Our kitchen door had a shelf at the top. You needed a chair to get things down). I would hold the bottle gingerly as if it were poison and hand it over to Grandmother. Then slid between her haunches. My arms flopped over her pulled-up knees. The brass cap never closed. It lost its fit when you opened the bottle, first time. Just made gritty noises as you turned the cap round and round. I had the brightest, sunburnt neck from the oil trailing down my neck. But my roots raced from the rancid coconut fix and tales of romance, piety and fear.

(iii) foully and the frosher

I am glad BhringRaj is not in the fetid bottle of my childhood. Even the cockroaches wouldn't go near it. For the environmental froshers with compost heaps in their backyards, who talk of homely lemon-and-sugar wax you eat as candy, as well as use to wax your legs, BhringRaj does its stuff. Liberates the froshers of deleterious chemicals. It even gives out a mighty pong when hair sweats. Such work inspires these earnestos, whose bodies are their temples and they pump their arms faster to the kicky fandango beat. It's Christmas! Big-time kicking and flying—Vegas showtime in an aerobic studio in northeast Calgary. BhringRaj, a signature in your gym bag:

You are bright about your body
You are bright about your environment

But like cinnamon-flavoured floss, the nineties' bottle *is* processed. It's translucent, way too bleached to hoard my Grandmother's stories, terrifying, and simultaneously, so upbeat. BhringRaj of the nineties is fetched in recycled aesthetics with a leak-proof coriander-coloured cap. Only, if you don't wash your sweaty hair after a workout, the rancid smell breaks out. I'd say, the Maharajah has teeth after all, toned down, but nonetheless, teeth, underneath his friendly-green literature on recycled Maa-earth plastics.

Just as the same-same skyscrapers have taken over the downtowns of Dar, Oslo, blah, blah, blah, there are the same-same homogenous green-soothers all over. Their boardroom members, exhaustive leaf-and-bean lifestylers who skin off stories with their unturned holistic power: earnest on the fallal, out of whack on the catgut. Stories which yank hair till it comes down, purple-black torrents of blushes are digested with shameless, undented innocence.

But I know what was passed to me on the verandah of my Grandmother's house, sitting between her haunches, my long hair untied, waiting. That waffling stories make hair grow: stories of basking morals, of harassment, of repayment and stashed desires, of revenge and dazzling scruples, stories of fear. Fear makes hair grow.

(iv) forget Deepak Chopra

Switch off Deepak Chopra. You don't need the la-di-da of a sesame oil message to hitch your spirit and body together. Nor the New Age doctor's ten steps to equilibrium. You know, your Grandmother knew, your great grandmother knew the goodness of a sensible red apple, and the art of pacing . . . with heart.

To my company of women, to you and I, *salut:*

Sway on your swing, sway on your porch, sway on your rooftop... your hair is wet and clean. (My lovely friend Amy used to wash her hair in the summer rain, and once the rain changed to hale. White nuggets in her hair, Amy started to run all over the house: back porch—front porch—upstairs—downstairs—laughing, clueless. Amy's rain.)

It's on porches (or swings or rooftops) that chores and messages and faxes and the traffic leave their shoes outside, as if it's the very mosque (this porch is your space or call it prayer). You watch the phone lines swing with plump motley dun-brown birds. The smell of date loaf in the oven glows things soft, even the scratches on the glass table.

There is an honesty you and I have mislaid perhaps, that honesty when things were wrapped in newspapers, when fingers smelt of bread and butter, when supper plates were white, when rice pudding was not a lost art, when Grandmother rubbed BhringRaj in your hair, when you never washed it plain dry, when raw mangoes were slit and pickled at home, when clothes were dried in the sun, when the moon of Idd was soft as mother's smell, when Allah was women's too, when the rise to prayer came out of your belly not a kalashnikov, when so many, many things were a treat and you biked about in one of your four cotton dresses, when children's cheeks and wrists were chubby a while longer, when your handshake was your seal, when you knocked on your neighbour's door thoughtless, just not during floods and quakes like on TV, when loving yourself, *valenting* yourself was a continuation, not a bestseller declaration . . .

When you and I come down to this honest, this un-rush you and I have mislaid, then the story of women's hair is also re(treat). Especially when newly washed. Hair drying on porches, verandahs, swings and rooftops. Women mull soft then, like the morning after throbbing sex. Some watch birds. Some catch the valentine of sounds. Some curl up, cheek pressed against the top of the sofa. Some switch off the TV, nose in coffee, letting the steam billow. Some do away with a towel, the small of their backs, a puddle. Some sing mute in their heads. Some sing smiley as teeth. Some curl their toes like it's the beach. Some down their toes to down a thought. Some relish the plain squeak of clean. Some remember the intoxication of titles, like "The Day I Sat with Jesus on the Sun Deck and a Wind Came Up and Blew My Kimono Open and He Saw My Breasts." Some pray just for the hell of it.

(v) some pray with skunk fear

For my Aunt, each pleasure is defensively moist as tears. She won't laugh with all her teeth. Just like it's precaution to call a pretty flower, chicken's toilet paper. To tone down, to distrust happiness. Yama of death doesn't turn up just once. Small deaths jump out all the time.

That's Yama on the tease. And each time, he takes a bite off you. My Aunt's favourite lines:

> sucking in daily breath, I know death
> I dare you to give me something larger

Her way of spitting on Yama.

Finally, finally, everyone in the family is on payroll again. My thankful Aunt fasts every Thursday—Allah, no more layoffs. She loathes contract deals, a bit here, a bit there. That's Yama: now you see him, now you don't. For my Aunt to be splendidly quenched (she will show all her stunning teeth) jobs must be steady, wide as feet. She prays, skunk fear in her heart, for anytime a job may be snatched. Her liver pounds. Pounds for her babies. She remembers those times, how she would wait on one leg: should she stop doing the dishes, put off slicing the onions until the children have finished with the job sections in the *Herald* and *Globe*? An itsy way she can cocoon them. Curb their stings, buffer that smashing laidoff workers endure (like a boxer's purple punch). These are her babies. Her lot as well as her sisters'. But all of them, largely hers. In Dodoma, she supervised their homework, made sure they learnt their timetables by heart. Now, in Calgary, she is shy (too shy) on the phone with strangers. She wasn't this way before—before, in Dodoma. Here, they say her accent is thick. In turn, her listening grows thick. It frustrates her babies when she transposes phone numbers. It's like you were a super driver in Tanzania. Bert Shankland of the East African Safari couldn't hold a torch to you, you would boast. You were cool on wobbly bridges, the ricketiest bends. In the whole of East Africa, they called you The Rift Valley Twister. Potholes and thickets of stars above were your traffic guides. You drove through the forest with full blast hunch and four pairs of eyes. Two in the front and two at the back. Then you come to Calgary and blunder a driving test on a road smooth as Alpha milk; the blasted traffic signs on poles, chatty bright as if there is a party on. Like the driver from Tanzania, my Aunt was the best—there. The best student, the best Girl Guide, and the best Mum-Aunt. But in Calgary, her confidence is blown out of its socket. It hovers over her like a ghost in bomb tatters.

For songs, stories and breasts beautiful as mangoes, us babies went to our other aunts, her sisters. But this Aunt-Mum, whose armpits smelt of onion soup regularly and cumin seeds when she made beef pilaff on Fridays, pulled us through timetables, algebra and logarithms. Under her quilt-but-fang eyes, we drank up our carrot juice, cleaned our nails, polished our Bata shoes last thing before bedtime, and swallowed our weekly quinine. When our legs hurt at night, she bandaged them with her husband's ties.

She watches her babies around the dinner table, engineers and teachers now. Jobless. She is banned from their punched adult dignity, beggar-rage silences. She watches them scan the papers with hot malaria eyes. Her hands waiting, a ready bib. They have to only eek out a sound, a scratch will do. Her babies are pieces of her very liver. But she can't say it to them. Mum is the word.

Every Thursday, her room smells of shampoo and incense. She dries pillow cases outside, pegs sprays of sage on them to bring the smell inside. Grateful for the kindness of daily things Yama hasn't snatched. Cross-legged on her bed, her hair dripping—when she talks to Allah, she likes the torrent of holy Ganges dripping down her back. Her Islam is not the monotheist kind, it has rivers, and trees and animals out of her Hindu lineage, from way, way back, when her great grandparents from Cutch were Hindus. She coaxes Allah to lighten her babies' loads. In Calgary, where business is still done at the kitchen table and language is ajar as the prairies, she has grown less formal, "Give them a break, will you," she tells Him. The small of her back flooded, warding, warding off Yama. Soulful, flooded Ganges at her side.

(vi) lemonading. also a kind of fighting back

Warming up "lucky:"

Finally, I leave Canada to teach in Chonju, Korea. Mr Chrétien, I can't live on reja reja—a paltry job here, a season there. So one day, Mr Chrétien, my palm itches real bad (right palm is even better) and Grandmother sighs. She sees one of my long trips coming. There goes her future three months, only this time I will be gone away for two years. Grandmother lies awake in bed, pulling in Allah with every bead on her *tasbhi*, wondering what mapless village her granddaughter is in today. She won't hear that Chonju has cappuccino and faxes. Anything beyond her bed is seven seas away. She is over eighty-five, Mr Chrétien. Also in Calgary, the righteous unemployment officer wouldn't take any balderdash from an artsy-fartsy cleaning up unemployment. Get a mop! That's how she filed me.

In Room 101, at Chonbuk National University, my homemaker students come across "luckiest." They suck in long breaths through their teeth. They are ticked off. They aren't interested in tough lessons on a Monday. They have had a terrorizing morning pushing soup into their kids' unbudging mouths and the husband won't deter from his morning ginseng and milk expectation. He just has to push the red button on the juicer. But he waits for his headless wife (that's how she feels), sucking his teeth, ticked off.

"Hey, but women, you know lucky . . . right?" I coax them. But they are a miffed lot and won't push the "Go" in their brains. So I jostle in an extra Monday shimmy in my eyes, in my armpits, the back of my knees. Shimmy Yasmin, shimmy, "Last night, I saw a huge, shiny, black pig in my dream!" My students whip into action, "*Waah,* you are lucky, lucky, lucky!" Gotcha! The word is a rosary: auspicious, hungrily desired: red is lucky and dreaming of a black pig means a son or winning a lotto. But "luckiest" is intimidating to the ear, so wordy on page—the English "est" and "tions" vexes them. In a repeat lesson, I make up a sentence: I feel I'm the luckiest person. I work by a lotus pond and my students are terrific (except on Monday mornings) and every four months I get to hop over to Bangkok, Panaji and Beijing.

"*Waah* Yasmin, we envy you!" Gotcha!

Lemonading, not lamenting:

It's holiday time again! I'm lemonading in Delhi. Yes, just that: while collecting unemployment in Calgary, I am invited to guest-edit a magazine out of Vancouver. I leap to the opportunity to work (my resumé would then confirm I wasn't goofing off watching Pakistani melodramas from Franklin Video) and to top it, in my field! Not waitressing or bugging people on the phone around supper time with shit merchandise. *Waah*, I am lucky, lucky, lucky. I hop on a plane to Vancouver for a three-day meeting and contract signing. When I return on Sunday, my answering machine beeps red flashes from the unemployment office. I whimper all night long. During interrogation (Monday morning, of course), the officer says this editing thing sounds wily-nily. So, I help her along, "You mean, like being by the pool, drinking lemonade?" The officer nods. Both her hands are on the top of her desk. She has nothing to hide. Her neat chestnut hair is side-parted (the only wanton luxury she allows herself). She is wearing a delicate gold watch (even has that thin chain drooping from its clasp) and her Sear's scarf is tied in a loose overhand knot. I know right off she has her date loaf down pat. Never over-moist or charred on top: a cup of boiling water to soak the dates *means* a cup of boiling water. This one will never go for pine nuts when the recipe calls for Safeway's walnuts. I give up. I move to Korea.

At Panjsheel Park in Delhi, I am lemonading *not* lamenting as my Word Perfect spell check offers—no way José: To shed off the *paleek paneer, Hydrabadi biryani,* chicken tikka, *shammi* kebabs, creamy *raajmaa* (just them beans, but what a luring name) and dripping buttered *naan*, I jog every morning in the colony's exclusive park. The first time I meet a peacock strutting towards me (it's an aggressive strut), I forget to relish its plumage and hop off to the side to inspect the neem trees. I even say "Hi birdy"—a nervous hello I croak out in the presence of a customs officer. Peacocks and customs officers have pellet eyes. Otherwise, I jog free and happy. Other joggers carry house keys and car keys and the grimace of determination. I get my second wind and fly. All 140 pounds of me. To hell with my wobbly bum. I am a streak of blue sky, a flash.

Fooding:

It all begins on the rooftop with a glass of fresh orange juice sealed with an upside down saucer. (The squeezer's palm marks the glass.) Of course, I never shove my food down but masticate delicately. Refined yellow stains on my index and middle fingers and thumb only. I eat chic. I eat barrels.

Junk is swell:

And read inconsequentials like "Double Happiness" in brilliant red and gold on a billboard at the Kai Tak Airport, Hong Kong. The advertisement is either for la-di-da cigarettes or a double bed. And absolutely nothing beats the nirvana of reading foreign weekend papers (you sit on the fence and titter or make aristocratic notes). Gin & Tonic by the side, 10 AM is swell.

*

Ah, I am moving my big toe in pleasure, titbitting on the butcher's *chitti* to his memsahib in the times of the Raj. I like to think this courtly butcher is from around Jama Masjid in Old Delhi, the hubbub of old Mogul polish. In his *chitti* to his dissatsfied memsahib, he hoits Plain Jane English with an Urdu flourish of nape bends and *"vous"* declarations to placate her, woo her back:

Honoured Madam,
Madam's butler say that
madam is much displeased with
their butcher because mutton too
much lean and tough. But sheep
no grass get, were get fat? When
come rain, good mutton. I kiss
your Honour's pious feet.
Your affectionate butcher
Mohammed Casseim

*

Here's another tickler: Upper-class Indians give their children avante garde names like Pinkie, Dimple, and this is a new one, Puppy! Personally, I still cannot get over the fact (and I read this ages ago, when newspaper sections had unspruced headlines like "Leisure" and not the electronic hip "Timeout") that Benezir Bhutto's pet name is Pinky (because she was such a pink baby). People in high stations choose meticulous partners to breed pink-and-white babies and give them daffy names.

Anecdote:

This exotic politician who wears a white dupatta on CNN with such demeanour. And speaks with classic simplicity, weight. *Waah,* I'm certainly razzmatazzed. But on an Indian telly, her arms thrash about, embarrassingly *jungly*, screeching at "The Indians dogs." On *Larry King Live*, Pinky or call her triple-scoop Baskin Robbins, Madam Politician flavour, is full of urbane Islamic panache. Naturally, Mr King is charmed nuts.

The tin with the black bottom:

Exercising, nourishing myself on Mogul dishes, and another abundant luxury of lemonading is I oil my hair, everyday. First, I heat Maharaj BhringRaj in a wobbly tin pot which I hold with a pair of kitchen pinchers. I don't think I am supposed to heat the oil in that pot because the bottom expands and becomes powder black in less than two minutes. So, once I carefully pour the heated oil in a saucer, I place the pot on a newspaper beside my Kiwi shoe polish kit (my shoes are damn shiny in Delhi). Basking and massaging my scalp without camel-stocked baggage of questions from Grandmother or my dear Aunt-Mum who never smiles with all her teeth:

(pry, pry, pry) "I heard you got a call today?"

(an immigrant's eternal timidity) "Take any job, it's a foot in the door."

(The finale, the everything-will-be-OK nugget—my biggest gripe) "Allah has everyone's name written on each grain of rice, not to worry."

Migrating to the rooftop to let my hair billow and fluff:

On a rooftop of the suite I have rented in this posh Delhi colony, I remove frail knots from my wet hair (just a tug, BhringRaj has made them limp), listening to melodramatic *ghazals* on my Sony Walkman. This one, sung by Jagjit, one of my all-time favourites:

If the word spreads, people will make it go far
they will slide
their own meaning
to your bone-dry hair
apply a new business to your shaking fingers

Gosh, and I take so much with me up on the rooftop: instant coffee (percolator drinkers don't understand the joy of boiled instant Nestlé coffee, milk and sugar), blue-bristled hair brush, writing book, a thicket of newspapers and good old vaseline for my heels.

For your eyes only:

Below, I can see the trees in Panjsheel Park. They are in tai-chi repose, slow and wide and bent at the trunk. The two small birds which usually sit on my ceiling fan in my room have flown to the rooftop, chattering sharply (we have a breadcrumbs alliance). Without warning, something soft mullies inside me like caramel on stove, a slow, slow fire. A yearn. I haven't prayed for ages. Can't. When an education minister says a woman is a rose, for your eyes only, and you must bolt her at home, and all these soldiers who have taken over on Allah's behalf in army struts, soldiers with inferno beards and Omar Khayyam eyes, I press my legs tight and my unhacked arms don't leave their precious sides.

Salute to a Filipino Girl:

I twist stories like my Aunt flips about phone digits. Amy, my dear friend, who used to wash her hair in summer rain and once in hail (that was a heady accident), cries "What!" to my rendition of Sarah Balabagan's story—I tell Amy that this sheikh, her UAE employer (but they are always some kind of a sheikh, aren't they?) well, his family is going to pay blood money to this Filipino girl who worked as a maid at their home. (I think blood money meant the blood her employer tore from her, forever.) The girl stabbed and stabbed him fresh. Amy says, "No, no *she* has to pay blood money to the sheikh's family because *she* killed him."

There is a girl who keeps hedging the pig, sending money home, apart and unshielded, barred from any rescue, quarantined from any rescue (who cares about domestics until they make headlines? Then grant them movie deals). But right now, this girl, Sarah Balabagan has just one thing: herself. She is fiercely brave. What flows between her legs is dark, private and hers. It's not up for abuse. If I keel, I want to keel on her banks. No, I don't twist her story. It's prayer. Not the downy kind with eyelids bent, but an invocation lunged with an eye-for-eye rage.

In the photograph in *Newsweek*, there is a policeman whose dark hairy arm is extended towards the ignition (behind his morning shaven face, has he also pillaged women?) Sarah Balabagan sits next to him. She is scratching the palm of her hand as if she can't remember her timetables by heart. Either Allah comes down and does some quadruple parting of a sea—something heavy-duty (men like the rush) to jostle an awakening in men or Muslim women like me walk out. Where the hell is my Allah of moon and henna and Friday beef pilaff and gestures of giving unshowy? And I am no rose to be stuck in a pot for anyone's eyes (not even Allah's), but I have a mother, a brother, my frightened

Aunt, and my Grandmother pulling her beads for me. Watch your tongue, watch your tonguc. Away from home, don't rouse His wrath. I leap off my buffy chair, charge down to my room to check my shoes. The two birds fly off in panic. Their tiny wings make an incredibly heavy whuump! as they cut close to my ear. I make very sure none of the shoes are upside-down, otherwise my mother dies. A superstition I haven't been able to shake off. Shouldn't have lambasted Allah. He only has to command Yama on the double. No, he won't. Yama is Hindu. But why take a fucking chance? For all I know, all gods up there might be one giant United Nations, padding about in their socks, pooling in. I am not ready to ask Allah's forgiveness just yet, so I dial and listen to the shrill of the phone. It's 2 AM at home. My skunk smell plugs the transmission lines all the way to Calgary.

Her Hair and Woman:

On my bed, I am stiff as sastrugi, even though I catch a whiff of the faint stink of coconut and terrace sunshine in my hair. My chums fly to the fan and I break some crumbs. I can't forget Sarah Balabagan. Travel pushes you to the edge. It's a kind of worship. You walk different. You eat different. Away from the stability of paying monthly utilities and carting groceries from Safeway to the car trunk, you send out feelers you never knew you had. You welcome differently.

Day in and day out, the girl scours and cleans and listens to the rapid pitiless orders of the women of the palace, shielding herself from their suspicious pellet eyes (of course they must know) and the shrill of spoilt kids who servant her around, and she with four eyes, two in the front and two at the back, sidesteps the leech with his unblinking prerogative and blind licence. In the end, she makes a regal choice. Sarah Balabagan. My long hair with its dark smoothness starts to warm the clamp around my neck, easing the packed rigidity to the sides, gently loosening it away. Sarah Balabagan.

Lemonading to be brave, skunk fear still in my heart:

I rock myself. I don't have beads, so I touch each half circle on my fingers, whispering Allah, Allah, Allah, killing two birds with a stone: lul-loving myself (Allah can't or won't) and thanking Him: "Keep my family safe. From thee is my strength and thou art my protection." It will be a long time before I pray just for the hell of it.

Liquid Seasons

SUNAINA MAIRA

There is rain, and then there is rain. I hate freezing drizzle on winter sidewalks, slippery slabs made resolute by snowstorms endured. I've never really liked March showers either, but at least they drench the skin with the titillation of sprouting green. And then, there are the monsoons, the rain-bearing winds I've heard of from my mother that assault the earth for months, seeping into the parched cracks of hungry earth, flowing through city streets in muddy brown rivers, beating down on roofs for days and days and days. A deluge would be depressing, but at least it would suffuse the air with sound; I wanted the sky to pour forth rhythm and thunder and liquid beats that give way to pauses of damp quiet. Boston swathed me in historic peals and powdery snow but it was always white noise. I wanted to hear traffic running through the night outside my window. So I moved to New York, two weeks after I graduated from college, with my futon, four crates of records, and two jars of my mother's homemade lime pickle.

When I stepped out into the languorous heat of the Manhattan summer and felt the heavy, humid air, it occurred to me that perhaps I was just another drop in the steady stream of eager young musicians and wannabe deejays that passed through this city in frustrated obscurity. I had only been here for three months, but already I was beginning to wonder if my decision to move here to get into the Indian music scene had arisen less from career ambition than from a fit of post-college confusion. My parents had, in their odd way, been surprisingly calm when I announced I was moving to the big city. They were far too preoccupied with the potential family scandal they feared would erupt when my sister turned thirty and remained blissfully unmarried. So my plans to go into the music industry seemed, by comparison, an innocuous obsession that would surely pass. I wondered if it had ever occurred to my parents that this was how they had always talked about my sister's lifestyle after she came out—a passing bout of waywardness that would subside with the help of time and vigilant protection from the corrupting influences of America, where depravation and debauchery curdled the rivers of milk and honey. Luckily for me, they didn't know much about Manhattan, let alone the West Village, so they were quite charmed by the leaf-shrouded street lamps and cobbled sidewalks in the area where I worked. I walked to the music store in a metropolitan daze, grooving to my favourite trance dub. My tiny studio in the crumbling walk-up seemed a spacious haven, the walls receding with the spreading relief of a guilt-free room.

When the humid air began to waft in from the sea, however, the city became unbearable. Traces left by dogs on the sidewalks floated up in putrid vapours, the steam from warmed concrete mixing with garbage and exhaust. At night I slept between two fans pointing at the bed but still the mattress clung to my back like a slab of soggy vinyl. At the store, the other deejays became crabby. I was morose, not having been able to get a single gig at any of the Indian parties that were springing up all over the city. This irony was brought home to me one day when I was sitting on a stool behind the cash register and DJ Sunshine walked in. I knew her instantly. Red baseball cap worn backwards, large eyes etched in black kohl against her sunburnt skin, and jeans so wide they made her tiny frame practically disappear. I scrambled off my stool, hitting my knee against the counter and knocking several records off the table.

DJ Sunshine didn't even blink. I fumblingly collected myself and the records and stared at her, groping for the right, career-sealing introduction.

"Hi," I said. "I'm Tahira."

"Yeah? I'm Sunny. I was wondering, do you have my CD in here?"

Somehow it hadn't ever occurred to the store owner, DJ Karma Cool, to ask me to recommend music that we should stock. I shook my head dumbly, my vision of spinning bhangra at the Banana Club on Friday night disappearing into a kohl black void.

"Well, I guess I'll be movin.' " DJ Sunshine grabbed her backpack and strode out the door, taking the last ray of my remixed, gold-shot fantasies with her.

"Sunny, Sunshine, wait! I love your music, I hear you on the radio every Friday, I just moved and . . . can I talk . . . " But the sticker-studded backpack was just another shaky blob in the shimmering afternoon haze.

That was the same day I first met Isabel Alvarez. I had gone up to Karma Cool's apartment, which was just above the store, to get his cellular phone for him. When I turned his key in the lock, a woman's voice called out from behind the door, "Quien es?" I was completely taken aback. Karma Cool had never said his girlfriend spoke Spanish.

"It's just me . . . it's Tahira from downstairs . . . I work in the store. Karma wants me to get his phone." I waited.

The door swung open. It took me a few seconds to get used to the dimness of the apartment, the black rug and black shades absorbing the little light there was inside. Isabel was standing near the entrance to the tiny kitchen, leaning on a blue-handled mop. Her hair must have been silver, because it gleamed softly, and there was something about the quiet, poised way in which she stood that made the mop handle look like an elegant lamp post.

"I'm sorry if I scared you," she seemed to have guessed that I didn't understand Spanish. Maybe she slipped into her mother tongue when she was alarmed, like my grandmother used to do with her alarmed "Tauba, tauba!" I was pretty taken aback myself. I had no idea that Karma hired a maid to clean his compact apartment. Lazy bourgeois pig, I thought, enjoying a sense of moral superiority over my boss.

"Hi, I'm Tahira."

Isabel took off a plastic glove and wiped her forehead with the back of her hand. Something about her face, the way her hair was parted in the middle and pulled back in a bun, seemed familiar. It suddenly struck me that she was wearing something startlingly like a salwar-kameez, the pink pallav tied efficiently around her waist, like nani did when she used to go for her morning walks in the summer—there I was thinking of my grandmother again. I was about to say something when Isabel switched on the kitchen light. The folds of her fuchsia skirt rippled as she bent down to squeeze the mop. I felt oddly disappointed and then a bit sad. I hadn't really thought about nani since she passed away last year, and it was strange to have these flashbacks now. It must be the heat, I thought, and the strange thin light inside.

"Want some tea?" Isabel asked. The familiarity of her tone washed over me, making me feel cosy and despondent at the same time.

"Sure, I'll get it. What the hell, I mean, so what, I don't have to rush down to work. Karma's probably still getting his frappucino."

Isabel laughed, and I began giggling too. We sat in the living room, Isabel sinking into the big black leather armchair, nervously at first, and then calmly swinging her legs up onto the leather footstool with a sigh. I giggled again.

Isabel arched an eyebrow over the steaming mug. "What do you do?"

"I, er, . . . " I looked into the glass coffee table and saw a small pale face, large raccoon eyes glowering at me. "I don't know what I want to do. I guess I moved to New York because I thought I'd get into the music world, you know. Indian remixes, that kind of thing."

"Are you Punjabi?"

I almost spilled my chamomile tea on the white rug. Jesus, how could she tell where my family was from originally?

Seeing my answer, Isabel said, "I know because my grandfather was Punjabi too. He came to California . . . oh, way back when, he was a farmer in the Imperial Valley. He grew peaches, then he moved into grapes in Fresno."

I put down my mug and stared at Isabel, barely-there muslin dupattas fluttering in the windows. I had heard about those North Indian men who travelled by ship, often boarding in Calcutta or other outposts of the British Empire such as Hong Kong, where they were stationed as soldiers or police officers. They came to Canada, and then to California, working on railroads, farms, and lumber mills.

Isabel went on placidly, "Then he married my abuela, she was Mexican. She left him, but came back a few years later. They kept fighting. My mother, Maria Singh, she married a Mexican. Grandfather was the one who walked out that time. Got drunk and almost fell down in the irrigation ditch, I heard." Isabel laughed, her teeth white against her golden brown skin. "He wanted his daughter to marry a rich Hindu farmer."

"Hindu?" My mother had told me Singh was a Sikh name. I remembered because she said it meant "lion," brave warrior from the Punjab.

"Oh, that's just what all the children called them. 'Hindu,' 'Hinda.' They were part Mexican, my mother and her friends, and they were very close to their Mexican mothers and godmothers. My mother was Catholic, and she knew my grandmother would stand up for her when she married Ramon Alvarez."

My mind was swirling, intoxicated by this unheard-of genealogy, a lineage bottled and kept away in an old cellar no one had bothered to tell me about. "There were other Mexican . . . Punjabi Mexicans?" Picking peaches together in the California sun, dreaming of rivers back home, of sisters and aunts fanning themselves on the verandah. I felt that twinge of missing someone again. Only now it was mixed with excitement. The summer was long, but there had been summers before this, drier, and longer.

"Oh yes, honey." Isabel got up and patted her bun. "We ate tortillas, you know, except we ate them like chapattis, with our hands." Isabel must have seen my eyes growing wide, because she continued, "We did the bhangra, too, except instead of . . . "

"Bhangra? You mean, Punjabi folk dance . . . like mixed with Mexican music or . . . ?" I could barely stop the beats from pounding in my head.

Isabel suddenly threw her head back and laughed, a very bubbly, tinkly laugh for a woman of her composure. I wasn't sure why she was so delighted. She turned to look at me, smiling, "Ay, chica, you love stories, I can tell." She rubbed her eyes, trying to wipe the amusement away. "Of course, we didn't eat chapattis, maybe some of the others did, but I never did any bhangra dance. My mother wanted me to be a good little Catholic girl—I wore frocks and took communion."

The fluttering white dupatta became a frilly confirmation dress, starched and white against brown skin. My daydreams were apparently transparent, that shimmering rope I wanted to tie between the continents my family had travelled, only Isabel had been skipping rope since she was a little girl, many, many years more than I had.

I saw her almost every other day after that first meeting. Karma Cool seemed to have become increasingly absentminded and was perturbed to find that when he thought his phone was downstairs, it was actually upstairs, and when his shades were meant to be in the apartment, they were suddenly missing and took ages to find. Isabel and I made iced tea and sank into the leather sofa and painted our toenails vixen red—I introduced her to Wine With Everything, with a clear topcoat. She smuggled in sangria one day and we talked about our fathers and the sound a door makes when it slams behind you in an empty room on a long, rainy night. I showed Isabel how to use a butterfly clip to hoist her hair above the dampness of neck. She braided my coarse waves, gently pulling tendrils over my ears and firmly tying them at my nape, her fingers brushing my shoulders with the lightness of certainty.

I thought at first that perhaps she had really become just another grandmother, or the mother I would have wanted to have, who knew what it was like to be brown in a schoolyard of white, yet who spoke in something other than English, who thought at a tangent to the straight line I had been taught in school. Was it so simple? I don't think so. And I don't think she wanted a daughter either. She told me once that she had never married because she didn't want to raise children in another home where someone was always leaving. Isabel never talked about why her own mother left Ramon Alvarez, but she said that she was very young at the time—she only remembered that her mother woke her up very early one morning and said that she didn't have to go to school that day, they were going to take the train all the way to San Diego.

"I missed the class picnic," she said. "I wanted to say goodbye to Papa, but Mama said that we were getting late, and that besides, he would probably be mad if we woke him up."

I thought of my sister Sarita in her apartment in San Francisco, writing newspaper articles three hours behind the East Coast light. Her girlfriend's voice always sounded so clear, so steady, when I called them, as if Sarita's nervous anticipation of the latest parental diatribe could only be balanced by Geeta's unwavering resolution. My parents always sounded relieved when they called and heard my voice on the other end of the line, as if they had expected someone else to pick up the phone.

Isabel would smile when I recounted these family entanglements, as if she were indeed listening in on the domestic drama on a second line and could hear every measured word. She said she was tired of cleaning up after Karma's parties, but she needed a break from California and had spent three weeks looking for a job after moving to New York. She missed her friends at the restaurant where she used to work in San Diego, but at least she could talk to me regularly. I kept thinking she must have understood what poured through the music I played, my latest salsa-bhangra mix blaring a cool, decadently airconditioned beat.

I'd given up on the New York club scene, but one day one of the other store assistants, Hector, happened to hear my new musical hybrid and thought it would be perfect at the Café con Leche night, famed for its Nyorican drag queen act. Then he introduced me to Sonia, who wanted me to spin at the Pink Cactus on Latin night, and I was soon coming home at three and four in the morning in the middle of the week, smoke and scat vocals clinging to my hair. I didn't have to get rent subsidies from my parents any longer and they were actually glad to hear that I was working—although I didn't tell them that I had been referred to in the *Village Voice* as the "new kid with the sexy Latin/Indian vibes who gets all the sisters grooving under the sheets." A couple of the sisters at the Pink Cactus made some gentle moves, and I had to play it carefully to keep my job, so I went to their after-hours parties and came home alone. Isabel knew I had stayed out late when I stumbled up the stairs to get some tea, and she always wanted to know if I had been listed in any newspapers again.

Since Karma had begun to retreat to his apartment in the afternoons to take airconditioned naps, Isabel and I began meeting in her apartment and we had dinner together or went for walks in the park two or three times a week. I was enjoying the city at last—the heat was bearable if you kept the fans going all day—and I loved my night job. Lying in my room in the early hours of morning, it occurred to me that I never did really think about the sounds of traffic outside my window because I was too tired. I still had this parched feeling, sometimes, but it wasn't just rain I wanted anymore. There was room in the elbow of the night to cradle another head, but I figured I was too exhausted and too busy.

When I think about it now, I shouldn't haven't been surprised at the way the summer ended. I had been so preoccupied with my own daydreams, and perhaps the dizziness of summer made me imagine phantoms, wavering mirages willed by my own thirst. I remember I hadn't had dinner with Isabel for a couple of weeks; Sarita had come into town with Geeta and they dragged me to the Pink Cactus every other night till I said it was interfering with my professional role and told them to find another club. I couldn't bear to see them, they fit together so perfectly and did everything in tandem, like a spoon and a fork.

One day after work I went up to Karma's apartment to ask Isabel to come with us to an outdoor concert. The door was open when I went in, so I should have realized that Karma was probably there, but I didn't hear any voices. The shades were still down, but there was a rustle in the bedroom and I saw the outline of a figure stretched out on the rumpled sheets. Isabel was standing in front of the mirror, zipping up her skirt. I could faintly see the white line of her bra across her back, her gray hair falling over her breasts. She saw me in the mirror and immediately raised her finger to her lips, turning softly and making a motion for me to wait outside. It didn't matter, because I was frozen, even though the air in the apartment felt warmer than usual. Isabel buttoned up her blouse methodically and tiptoed past the sleeping Karma, shutting the door behind her.

For a moment I saw her standing there with the blue mop, like I did the first day, and I realized now that what I should have seen in the coil of her hair at her nape, what I should have sensed in the lightness of her fingers. She probably liked the pulse of Karma's music—the two-timing bastard—as much as I did. I felt a weird tug inside me again as I looked at her, but this time it was not sadness or wishfulness but something else altogether—the slow spreading clarity of remembering something you'd almost forgotten, finally sharpening the outlines of your waking dreams.

That night, I thought of taking a trip to California. I didn't care if it rained or not, and I wasn't afraid of El Nino's torrents, but I thought it would be nice to actually see Isabel's home rather than just fantasizing about it. I'd like to live somewhere for a while, not just move from one place to another, and get a real bed, maybe a queen size, who knows? I lay awake, hearing the rumble of the train as it rushed below the dusty, stained streets and then finally burst above ground on tracks shooting away from the city. There must be train tracks stretching across the entire length of the United States all the way to California, pikes struck into red earth by brown hands brought from Asia. Ships leaving San Francisco Bay for Hong Kong, turbans turned to the gray Pacific, watching the currents flowing, backwards now, to the Bay of Bengal, back to the shouts on the docks in Calcutta. When the monsoons break, the rains will lash the piers where the men had waved goodbye to land and drench their fields at home. The men feel the hands of their wives, the fingers of their lovers, wiping the drops of sweat gently from their backs. Sometimes they caress in Punjabi, and then sometimes the strokes are in Spanish. It has been a long, hot, humid summer floating between shores.

Friends

FARIDA KARODIA

Hiroko and I met at a Christmas Eve party at Mary's place. Mary and Hiroko both worked at Arctic Gear, a company manufacturing skiwear. I had met Mary through Janice, an accounting clerk at Tower Oil and Gas, where I was employed as a receptionist.

Janice was one of my first friends in Calgary. She was Jamaican and, although she'd been in Calgary for fifteen years, had retained her distinctive Jamaican accent and her outrageous sense of humour. She had an easy way about her and was quick to laugh, except when she encountered incidents of racism. On those occasions according to Mary, she went "ballistic."

Mary once accused her of being overly sensitive, of picking up racial slurs in every comment. If anyone else had said this to Janice, she would have been down their throats, but since she and Mary had been friends for years, there was a good deal of give-and-take between the two. "What do you know?" Janice asked Mary. "When was the last time someone asked you where you come from? You're no hyphenated Canadian like the rest of us. Let me tell you, girl," Janice said bristling, as Mary and I exchanged alarmed glances. "You need one helluva thick skin to survive not only the cold in this place, but also the racism. Bloody bunch of rednecks. Every time someone run out of insults, or they see you not caring about what they say, they tell you go back to your own country. Christ, girl! This is my country. I'm a citizen and not some welfare bum like most of them come from Europe and not speak one word of English."

"Ignore them," Mary said calmly.

"Easy for you to talk. You got that lily-white skin, honey. Look at me. We as different as night and day." Janice found her own analogy hilarious and laughed.

"And I thought I left apartheid behind me," I said, adding my little comment.

"Uh, uh. No matter how long we live here. Whether we be third or fourth generation Canadians, you always be asked the same question—'where you from?' I usually say, 'I'm from heaven, honey. Where you from?' That shuts them up," Janice said, laughing again.

Janice was not going to Mary's Christmas Eve party. She was taking her two kids to visit a relative in Edmonton. Melissa was nine and Eric six. Janice had raised both children on her own when her husband ran off with a "white" girl. "White trash," was the way Janice referred to the woman.

Before Janice left for Edmonton, I consulted her about a gift for Mary.

"Booze," she said. "Booze is always a good idea."

I took a bottle of wine.

My first Christmas in Canada was spent alone in my small apartment, watching TV and feeling pitifully sorry for myself. While hoarfrost turned the city into a fairy land, I cried myself to sleep, vowing that I would never spend another Christmas alone.

I arrived at Mary's place in a taxi. The house was brightly lit and cheerful, a dramatic contrast to my dingy apartment. Mary's three-bedroom bungalow was on a pie-shaped corner lot, wide-end at the front and all of it frosted with at least two feet of powdery snow. The front porch was decked with strings of light. Amidst an assortment of Christmas decorations, a huge plastic facsimile of Santa perched incongruously on a rocker on the verandah.

The blue spruce in the front yard was draped in a mantle of fresh snow weighting down the branches. Huge globs of snow slid off and plopped to the ground in large wet chunks. Next door, the neighbouring kids frolicked in the snow—one of them, a little girl, was lying on her back making snow angels.

Mary met me at the door. She took my coat and the bottle of wine and waited while I removed my snow-covered boots and placed them with others in a rubber tray already holding a puddle of melted snow. I slipped into a pair of dress shoes brought along for the occasion and followed Mary through the carpeted living room to the rumpus room downstairs where the revelry was well under way.

An enormous Christmas tree, almost to the ceiling, stood in a corner next to the bar.

"Everyone, this is Helen," Mary said, tossing the introduction into thin air.

Someone responded, "Hi, Helen!"

In the corner, pressed up against an eager young woman, panting as though he had just run a marathon, a middle-aged, paunchy man glanced up with glazed eyes. A square of bare floor had been cleared and several dancers gyrated to some secret rhythm in their heads. Conversation was impossible above the blare of the stereo.

I smiled and edged towards the bar. From this vantage point I casually observed the guests. A young man, tending the bar, handed me a rum and coke.

After dancing with a man who was well on his way to passing out and had left me limping, and another who had burdened me with details of his unhappy marriage, I was quite content to watch from the sidelines.

In the far corner, Hiroko, small and almost waiflike, was comfortably ensconced in an armchair. Other guests sat on metal folding chairs. I noticed the way Hiroko's glance drifted around the room, carefully scrutinizing faces, especially those of the men.

She looked up, caught my eye and smiled sheepishly.

I eventually joined her, perching on the footstool, which she obligingly relinquished. Despite the noise, we managed to exchange bits of information about ourselves.

At eleven o' clock, Mary summoned us upstairs. More people were arriving. We donned coats and boots and joined a group of carollers gathered outside at the corner. It was minus twenty-nine outside and I thought of the contrast with back home in South Africa where friends and family had probably celebrated Christmas day with a *braai*—a barbecue.

After the carolling we returned indoors and gathered in the rumpus room where pitchers of hot rum drinks were served. Hiroko and I found each other again. I spoke in simple sentences in deference to Hiroko who claimed her English was not "very good."

She told me she had spent three Christmases in Canada, but this Christmas Eve party was her first. It was not for lack of invitations, she assured me, but more from a lack of will to go out on her own. Towards the end of the evening she unabashedly admitted, "I would like to find a husband." After a thoughtful pause and with a reflective sigh, she went on, "It would be much easier to live here with a husband—a Canadian husband. I want to be Canadian so bad, I can die," she said and with a wistful sigh, turned away.

The boldness of this confession—to me—a stranger, was surprising.

"I'm glad you're here now," she continued. By this time she knew that I was on my own, too. "You and me, we can be friends. We can go places together."

I nodded noncommittally, averting my eyes. I didn't want to be pinned down. Who knows, I thought, I might need a friend, or I might not. And if I did, it might not be Hiroko.

A group from our office had organized a skating trip to Lake Louise. The bus was to pick us up at seven in the morning. It was after midnight and I was bored and desperate to escape the party. I found Mary and made my excuses.

Hiroko looked a little disappointed that I was leaving early, but we exchanged phone numbers and promised to call one another.

A week later Hiroko called me. I agreed to go to a movie with her that same evening. While we waited in the cinema for the movie to begin, I related my adventures at Lake Louise. It was my first experience on skates and I had fallen so hard that I thought I had cracked my tailbone.

"After that fall," I told her "I tied a pillow around my rump."

"A pillow?" she asked, looking perplexed.

"Yes, I must have looked like a hippo." I expected laughter. The girls at work had lampooned me about the pillow.

At first Hiroko looked at me blankly. When she finally understood, the story was no longer funny.

Hiroko called regularly, asking me to accompany her to one place or another. I often made lame excuses. There were times when trying to communicate with her about anything other than the basics was just too exhausting. I had a much better time with Janice, even though babysitting problems usually required the inclusion of her kids in our plans.

I eventually gravitated towards Hiroko. She at least was available. Although I knew many people, I had few friends. Most of the women at work had other interests: boyfriends or families.

In winter Hiroko was frequently ill. She was delicate and prone to illnesses, especially colds and flu. I did not have a car. Taxis were expensive and the bus service then was not efficient. Going out in winter required exceptional effort and I was often too tired to care. After work I preferred to curl up with a book or watch TV.

When the weather improved Hiroko and I got together again. Hiroko was like a sponge. She wanted to absorb everything Canadian, but because of the diversity of the population, it was hard to figure out what was truly Canadian. Canadians themselves battled with this question, and of course we as newcomers had none of the answers. Undaunted, however, Hiroko adopted whatever she considered Canadian. She picked up the Canadian speech patterns and spoke with a comical mix of Japanese and Calgary influences. Barbecue, she decided, was truly Canadian, as was country-and-western music.

Hiroko, still insecure about her English, asked me to tutor her. We did this twice a week, Hiroko coming to my apartment after work. I understood her difficulty with the language. Even I, a native English speaker, had to reflect on the differences of pronunciation and expression. I could imagine how difficult it was for Hiroko to understand Janice, who spoke rapidly and with a Jamaican accent, her expressions often confounding me too.

Hiroko found Janice overbearing. Janice's bombastic manner intimidated her.

"Janice is like that," I explained one day when Hiroko and I went for a walk. "But she's a great person. She has a heart as big as a house." For a while Hiroko did not say anything, merely scuffed the toe of her runner in the sand as though trying to find the appropriate words. "I don't understand what she say to me. I think she laugh at me." The comment was obviously made with great difficulty because Hiroko never criticized anyone.

"She doesn't laugh at you, Hiroko."

"I don't understand her," she insisted.

"But you understand Hans, and he is German," I said sharply. Hans was one of the owners of the factory where she worked.

"He speaks slowly. He know my English is not so good."

"Hiroko, there's nothing wrong with your English. It's better than you think." I could see by the way her eyes swept past me in a large arc, that she was not convinced.

The friendship between Janice, Mary, Hiroko and me carried on through its high and low cycles. Janice and Hiroko never really got along and merely seemed to tolerate each other.

Then Hiroko met Douglas and the dynamics of our friendship shifted. I always knew that Hiroko would find a man—a Canadian. She was still obsessed with "things Canadian."

Hiroko and Douglas met at Arctic Gear. He had come to see Hans about something and Hans told Hiroko to measure him for a jacket.

It might have been while Hiroko was measuring Douglas that he flirted with her, but whatever the case, Hiroko was smitten. She went about dreamily. She told me she was in love. It happened, she said, the moment Douglas walked through the door at Arctic Gear. How naive, I thought, pityingly. But Hiroko, from that moment on, lived and breathed Douglas.

After several months of curiosity about him, I finally had the opportunity to meet him at her place one afternoon. I had heard that he was a cattle rancher's son from High River, a small town south of Calgary, a rugged cowboy type who did the rodeo circuit.

He was good looking, but cold and distant. Some women might have found his disdainful attitude appealing. I didn't. Hiroko emitted a glow that enveloped her like an aura. It softened her and in his hands she was as pliable as putty.

I studied him covertly, taking him apart—feature by feature, searching for flaws in the weakness of his chin, the softness of the upper lip concealed beneath a moustache. But his face was strong and angular and there were no apparent flaws, except for the eyes. There was something peculiarly disconcerting about his brown eyes, which seemed to undress women at a glance—even in the presence of Hiroko. Mary thought he had fascinating eyes. I thought they were just downright sly and calculating.

I did not like him. I was frank enough to tell Hiroko so afterwards when she asked me what I though of him. She laughed, dismissing my criticism, but was obviously hurt. Once when we had a row about something totally unrelated, she told me I was jealous of her relationship.

According to Janice, if you want something badly enough, you'll get it.

Hiroko got Douglas. She immersed herself in Douglas to the exclusion of all else. I couldn't help reflecting on how incompatible the two of them were.

Janice met him for the first time at the Ranchman's Inn, when he and Hiroko stopped in for a few drinks. Janice remarked that he was disgustingly macho. "I must admit, he's got a nice butt, though," she said as we watched Douglas striding away from our table. "Look at him strut. He's just full of it, isn't he?"

A few minutes later, watched by a pained Hiroko, he was on the dance floor with a blonde. Hiroko still thought the sun rose and set upon Douglas.

By this time we were already drifting apart. A few times when I called, Douglas answered and I put the phone down without speaking.

That summer, Douglas was riding in the rodeo at the Stampede and Hiroko phoned me. She desperately wanted to see Douglas in the calf-roping and bull-riding events but did not want to go on her own. She wanted me to go with her. I had seen the stampede events advertised on TV and could not imagine Hiroko in that kind of setting.

Despite my better judgement I gave in and reluctantly agreed to accompany her. It was raining that day. One could always count on rain over Stampede. Hiroko and I joined the throngs, dressed like every other stampeder—in western gear. Hiroko had bought a cowboy hat for the occasion and padded it with newspaper to keep it from sinking over her ears. Nothing could deter her. She was thrilled with everything. But after a few hours, I was exhausted and sick of being dragged from one event to another by an exuberant Hiroko.

We joined the crowd at the bull ring where she waited to cheer

Douglas. The contestants were ankle deep in mud and the bucking bulls kicked up globs of mud, drenching spectators around the enclosure. The rain was coming down in a steady drizzle and I had had enough of the Stampede.

"I don't know what she sees in him," I said to Janice a few days later. Occasionally she, Mary and I still got together for a "ladies' night." This was one of those nights and we had decided on the Keg & Cleaver on 10th. It wasn't one of our more successful evenings. Mary, who had had a spat with her boyfriend, was morose and uncommunicative. It was obvious that by the time we met at the Keg, Mary had already knocked back a few drinks. We listened to her complaints about her relationship and the conversation turned to men—and specifically to Douglas.

"Sometimes the most unlikely people get together," Janice said when I expressed my concerns.

"Look, can either of you imagine Hiroko spending the rest of her life with this guy? And what about the gun rack at the back of his truck? Hiroko hates guns. What's going on with that woman?" I asked.

Mary laughed. "He might have other attributes we can't see at a glance," she said, winking mischievously.

"Sex, isn't everything," Janice replied. "It's great, but you can't build a relationship on that alone. You gotta have other stuff too. Ask me. I know."

"Sex, my darling," Mary said, lighting a cigarette and blowing her smoke at the ceiling, "especially good sex, is the glue that holds couples together."

"A bull rider with Hiroko," I added, shaking my head in disbelief. "That's not glue, that's masochism."

The two women exchanged glances and Janice guffawed.

"Come on, Helen. Maybe it won't last. Stop behaving like a mother hen," Janice said.

"I think Hiroko knows a good thing when she sees it," Mary added.

"Yeah," Janice said dryly. "He probably doesn't have to put a sock in it."

The two laughed uproariously, while I mused about the oddness of this couple. "Hiroko is serious about the man. She's already planned the wedding and decided how many kids they're going to have."

"She wants to be Canadian," Janice said dryly. "What could be more Canadian than running around with the likes of Douglas?"

That night we talked about Hiroko and Douglas as though we had nothing else to talk about. We dissected their relationship and examined it minutely under a microscope. Focusing attention on Hiroko and Douglas seemed to provide a diversion for Mary and her personal agony.

Later that year, Hiroko went home to visit her parents in Japan. She was from a small canton near Kobe and had gone home to break the news of her engagement to Douglas.

I didn't know about the engagement until after the fact. I suspected that her parents' disappointment would be enormous. She was their only daughter and they had hoped she would return to Japan to marry a man of their choice.

There was no way any of us could extinguish Hiroko's passion for Douglas. He was her fantasy-come-to-life. What puzzled me, however, was Douglas's interest in her when he could have had any woman he wanted.

The two, as far as I could see, were totally incompatible. Hiroko wanted a home and family and Douglas was a drifter, living out of his truck, taking women at will whenever and wherever he wanted.

Hiroko returned from Japan as determined as ever to be with Douglas, despite her parents' objections.

Two months after Hiroko's return, she invited me to witness their marriage in front of the justice of the peace. Afterwards there was to be a small gathering, with no more than ten people, at a restaurant.

I was invited and so was Mary. I was disappointed that she had not asked Janice. Douglas's parents were there and although they were pleased that he was settling down and said this often and unselfconsciously, I could see that they too were perplexed by his choice. Nevertheless, they fussed about Hiroko. She beamed at them, radiant with happiness. I watched all of this surreptitiously, straining to look pleasant for her sake.

She smiled at me, as if to say, "What do you think now?"

Two of Douglas's brothers were present with their wives. All of them lived in and around High River. The wives behaved quite indifferently towards Hiroko, but Hiroko didn't seem to notice. She was too busy being happy.

Hiroko moved to High River. By this time I had bought a car and managed to visit her a few times. Once I persuaded Janice to go along with me. Janice was not too thrilled with the idea, but the kids were away visiting in Edmonton and so she agreed. Although surprised to see Janice, Hiroko welcomed her as though she were a long lost relative.

Janice and I were both astonished that Hiroko had slipped so easily into this rural way of life. She had become a typical farm wife: cooking, baking and sewing. She had put on weight and her face had plumped out. Douglas was not home. I had not encountered him on any of my previous visits either. Janice asked her if she was happy.

"I am very happy. I love Douglas. His parents they love me. They are so nice to me. So kind," she said, giving Janice and me a brilliant smile.

Janice's brow moved imperceptibly as she glanced at me.

Hiroko and Douglas lived in a mobile home set on an acreage. It had two bedrooms, a large living room, a bathroom and a kitchen. Hiroko had made the place as warm and comfortable as she could.

She had painted the place herself soon after she and Douglas moved in. On my third trip, there were more improvements: new curtains and a flower garden in the front. Now she proudly showed Janice and me around. She told us that Douglas had promised to build a deck.

Janice and I agreed that it was a lovely place. It faced west and from her windows she had a clear view of the mountains. In the distance two horses grazed in the pasture.

"Now Douglas is married, he get his share of the farm," Hiroko said. Suddenly the pieces clicked into place. I was so indignant I didn't dare look at Janice for fear of betraying my thoughts to Hiroko. On the way home, though, I vented my feelings. "The scoundrel. Can you see why he married her?"

"Sure I can, honey. He has obviously used her because he felt he could manipulate her."

"How can she put up with it?"

Janice shrugged. "Some women, they don't mind."

"I would never let it happen to me."

Janice opened her eyes wide as she gazed at me.

"What?" I asked, aggrieved by her expression.

"When you in love and you're burning with passion for your man, you don't even think about the way he treating you."

"Rubbish!"

"Uh, huh," she said, looking at me and smiling in that enigmatic way of hers. "You obviously not been in love yet."

I didn't see Hiroko for several months over the winter. She was married for a year already and was expecting her first child.

I went out in the spring to see her and the new baby. Hiroko showed me the crib she had found in a junk store and which she had lovingly restored and upholstered. The baby, with Hiroko's eyes and nose, kicked contentedly in the crib.

"I made many friends here," Hiroko said. "I'm quite happy now."

"What is Douglas doing?" I asked.

"Douglas is working on the family farm. I told you he have his share of the ranch now. His own cattle. He comes home very late. Sometimes he too tired to come home."

I didn't say anything. I suspected, however, from the way Hiroko's eyes clouded over as she tried to explain all of this to me, that something was wrong.

"Douglas hurt his back. Maybe soon as he's better, he'll build the deck," she said.

A few days later, I saw Douglas in downtown Calgary. He was just getting out of his truck, showing no signs of the bad back Hiroko had claimed for him.

The following week when I met Mary and Janice, I told them about my visit to Hiroko, her excuse for Douglas—his bad back—and then my seeing him in town.

"She going to learn the hard way," Janice said.

"The two of you are always looking on the dark side of everything,"

Mary scolded. "Maybe the man is working hard."

"Oh, yeah," I remarked sarcastically.

"I been to visit her already. You know I ain't one of her favourite people," Janice said.

"Nonsense," I protested.

Janice gave me the eye and I shut up. "Why don't you go see her, Mary?" she asked.

Mary didn't say anything. Then a few weeks later she told me she had taken a drive out to High River on a Sunday afternoon and had stopped in to see Hiroko.

"What did you think?" I asked.

"She was crying. She said she hardly ever gets to see Douglas. To crown it all, she's pregnant again. That's all he seems to come home for. He sold his share of the farm. The poor woman has nothing. She depends on his parents for support. I feel sorry for her. This is the way her life is going to be forever, unless she does something about it."

We felt sorry for Hiroko, but there was little we could do. Hiroko was proud and stubborn. In her quiet way she could be as immovable as the Rockies.

I would have gone out to see her again, but my car started giving me trouble. I called a few times to chat and always got the same reassurances from her when I asked her how she was doing.

Eventually like two leaves pulled apart in a current, we went our separate ways.

A year later I was offered a teaching position in Golden, a small town nestled in a valley on the Columbia River, just beyond the Kicking Horse Pass. I had taught for many years prior to coming to Canada and had struggled, quite unsuccessfully, to find a teaching post in Calgary. When I was offered this position, I took it immediately.

In August I left for Golden to find accommodation and settle in before the school year started. I found an apartment and had my few belongings moved in a rent-a-truck. My friendship with Janice continued and we spoke on the phone often. When I was settled comfortably, she drove out to visit with the kids. Hiroko's name, of course, cropped up and I asked Janice whether Mary had heard from her again.

"You know Mary. She not one to interfere in someone else's business," Janice told me.

"Never mind, I'll write to Hiroko. I have her address."

I was sad when Janice left Sunday afternoon; we'd had such fun. It was a three-and-a half hour drive to Calgary and she wanted to get home before dark. She assured me she'd be back soon.

A month later I wrote to Hiroko.

I never got a reply.

Three years passed and my life took so many different and surprising little twists that I rarely gave Hiroko any thought. I loved Golden. For the first time since coming to Canada, I felt as though I was part of the community. I made friends and started a new life. I could not have been happier.

My trips to Calgary became infrequent. Although the scenery was magnificent, I hated driving through the mountains. The Kicking Horse Pass was notorious for the number of lives it claimed. The road was dangerously narrow and winding with unexpected rock slides. On the other side only a flimsy barrier separated car and driver from the dizzying depths of a seemingly bottomless valley.

In the years I spent in Golden the clatter of the emergency rescue helicopter always caused a flutter in my chest.

Late one Saturday afternoon in December, we heard the helicopter taking off and the chilling sound of the ambulance siren. I wondered what poor victim had again been sacrificed at the base of the mountain. We usually heard about these events through the grapevine long before they were reported in the local weekly paper on Mondays. I listened for the returning ambulance, but there was no siren and I assumed that there had been no survivors.

Later that night I caught the tail end of a news bulletin about the accident. A woman and two children were killed instantly when their car went out of control and plummeted down the ravine.

Sunday morning, for want of something to do, I took a drive and passed the gap in the barrier. I slowed and peered over the edge. The car, crushed beyond recognition, still lay at the bottom of the ravine—half buried under a fresh fall of snow.

Monday I read that the car had landed on its roof and that the rescue teams had upended it to retrieve the bodies. All three, the mother and her two children had been killed instantly. The youngest was four. Names of the victims had not been released yet.

We talked about the accident at school. The deaths of children always seemed to touch a chord in people. I felt guilty that I, out of macabre curiosity, had driven out there to look at the grisly scene.

Later that night Janice called.

"You won't believe what I have to tell you," she said. From her tone, I could sense that something was wrong.

"What is it?" I asked, my heart doing a little flip.

"You know that accident, just outside Golden . . .?"

"Yeah," I said cautiously.

"It was Hiroko and her two children."

"What!" I gasped. "Are you sure? Where did you hear this?"

"It was in the Calgary paper. I just saw it. They gave the names. She must've been on her way to see you, girl. She left a note for Douglas to say she was going away with the children. Maybe she was going to leave him."

Pausing for a long moment, I struggled with this startling news. "Why didn't she phone to let me know she was coming?"

There was silence at the other end and I waited impatiently for Janice to respond.

"I don't know. A neighbour said she was quite desperate," Janice said quietly.

I sat, searching for words to express my grief. "Poor Hiroko," I muttered. "If only she had called on her friends."

"You know how hard it was for her to swallow her pride. The funeral is Friday. I heard her parents are coming."

"They must be devastated," I said. "She's the only child and they didn't approve of the marriage in the first place."

Janice was silent for a moment. Then she asked, "What about you, are you coming?"

"Of course," I muttered. "Have you told Mary?"

"Yes. I phoned her. She'll be at the funeral."

"You're coming aren't you?" I asked her.

After a small hesitation she said, "We weren't very close and I don't like funerals.''

I didn't say anything and she sensed the reproach in my silence.

''Okay,'' she muttered. ''I'll see you there. I suppose it's the least I can do.''

I put the phone down. Images of the gap in the barrier and the car lying at the bottom of the ravine ran through my mind and I thought of Hiroko's words: ''I want to be a Canadian so bad, I can die.''

By Lake Mendota

MEENA ALEXANDER

I opened her closet, pushed aside a packet of needles, a silver goblet. And there it was, under a pile of folded silk, a green-backed journal. So I stole her journal. Rather I took it away without telling her. Perhaps if I had asked her, she would have let me, who knows?

I sit with it at the water's edge. Lake Mendota. Fall leaves slipping gold and red onto the clear water. A wave or two, that's all, and the sky in the middle of earth—the mirror of heaven, isn't that what a lake is called. Didn't she tell me that?

Her journal is green, with stitching on the edge. Dull green as if it had weathered too much, sun, monsoon rain, dust from the small town in which she lived before coming to America.

I told Eric I was going to the lake's edge to read Mama's journal. He nodded, as if it were a simple thing, like having a cup of cider. Then ran his fingers through his hair, staring at me. Yasunari called him away. They were off to see the waterfall at the edge of the creek.

"Just discovered it," Yasu told me in great excitement.

They do a lot together, Yasu and Eric, particularly when Eric's work, on wind tunnels, the speed of water, meteorological data, is going badly. Imagine trying to make a science of matter that slips, slides, changes. It gives him headaches sometimes. Other times Eric laughs as if his soul were all filled with sunlight. He has dark eyes, small hands. Eric's mother is part Japanese and Yasu is his mother's second cousin, third generation from the Seattle area. They've been here a long time, not like Mama, who came full grown, met Papa in a coffee shop in Rye, moved to the city, had me.

"See you tonight," Eric waved.

Yasu was staring at the notebook in my hand, but said nothing. Some words came into my head, as I watched them set off, a single hand raised between the two of them, the trees green with moisture, and behind it all the waters of the lake rising.

Not waving, but drowning.

Where did that line come from? Why does it come to me?

Its not the kind of line Mama would write. Writing came to her with great difficulty. There were months when she couldn't write a single letter home. It was hard to understand Mama, but sometimes it was almost as if a single syllable sent home would tear her apart. As if she had to stretch her own substance so fine, to pass it through the hazards of crossing, faulty airplanes, bomb threats, trains threatened by high water, a postman, his bag sodden with monsoon rain. Why couldn't she just write a few lines on one of the flimsy air letter forms she hoarded? I wasn't ever sure. But she tried to explain it to me, draw me into her difficulties:

"Dora, I can't write home to my own mother."

She stood there with a kitchen knife, peeling potatoes for french fries, running the cold water over the thick brown skins. French fries and spaghetti and meatballs were the only American foods she was comfortable with. She needed help from me:

"Will you draw a picture, Dora, I can send your grandmother in India?"

When I said nothing, she went on: "Please."

I shook my head till my two braids flew into my eyes, blinding me. I had no interest in my Tiruvella grandparents. But a few days later, after feeding my guinea pig with raw cabbage I got from the salad Mama was cutting up, I opened my new box of crayons and made a picture. I checked with her first.

"A lady getting into an airplane. Is that OK?"

She perked up at that. "Of course darling."

"I'll make the sky blue."

"Blue." She echoed the word.

She stroked my hair as she saw the picture I made on the new drawing book Grandma Muriel had bought me. A lady in a sari with a big black bag in one hand. In the other, she held onto a little girl who had two long braids. They were going up the steps of an airplane. The steps were outlined in red. Around the plane, there was blue sky. Bright blue crayola in stripes. And stars. She liked that. Stars in a blue sky. Sun too. So the sun and the stars shone on that lady holding the little girl by the hand and the two of them got into the shiny airplane.

But later, angry with her for wanting to tear me away from Rosie and Jennie and Wanda, away from summer camp and hot dogs and pizzas, streets full of girls jumping rope by their stoops, I had a dream. That the shiny clocks and clothes and chocolates, tubes of saffron and skin cream and shampoo that she had bought so carefully to take back to India had all transformed. When she stepped out of the plane and opened up the black bag, it was full of rotten tomatoes, shrivelled purple cabbages, blackened onions. They oozed a stenchy liquid. She screamed as I stood in the airport lobby, staring at my shoes, saying nothing. Nothing at all.

Perhaps I took her journal because she wouldn't talk to me. Could tell me nothing. After all I needed to find out what I could about her and Papa, their breaking up. It was my life too. At least this is what I told myself. But then I wasn't so sure about rights in the matter.

There wasn't much in the journal: blank spaces with doodles, shopping lists, Papa's darjeeling tea, mild shampoo for my hair, and then, after a few pages a single line:

Went and sat with him by the water's edge.

I read those words and a curious disturbance filled me. As if sweet water from the depths of Lake Mendota had poured into me, filling me up like a jug. And someone had taken the jug and shaken it so harshly water turned brown as it churned.

A dark girl stood over me, her hair tight in two braids. She was shaking the jug, shaking me so hard, I wept to be let go.

I dropped the notebook on a flat stone by the tree. I raised myself. I strained my eyes so that I was looking as far away as possible. Further than where I thought the shore might be. Across grey water, the colour of goose feathers, the sky tilted.

When I was able to wipe my eyes free of wind and water, I found the page again. Or had the wind blown the pages loose?

The line looked a little different.

Met in Union Square. The ground was wet.

I stopped there. The wind was blowing hard. I could not read any more. Dark green ink, the colour Mama always used, comes off on my hand. I have a dark green patch of ink on my palm, shaped like a fig leaf.

The plastic ink bottle stood at the edge of the refrigerator, squat, oddly shaped, a household god. It was if she needed to see the ink bottle even in the kitchen, somewhere out of the corner of her eye. Or had she just stuck it there, unsure about what to do? Mama was dressed in her pale green sari with the reeds painted on the border, leaning over the stove with the burning fire in it. She had neglected to set the kettle right and the flames were naked, almost in her belly. Her torso was slightly twisted to the right, so she could stare out of the small window that gave onto the apartment courtyard, see blackened walls, flat roof, the pallor of sky. She stared and stared as if searching for some sign.

"Mama, Mama," I cried, tugging at her sari.

I was taller than the top of her thighs. My black braids bounced against my neck. When shc didn't respond, I picked up the outer edge of the wafting green sari and crept down low so I was the size of a small animal. I loved the warmth of her, as I hovered inside my mother's clothing. Slowly, her hand came down and groped for my head. Stroked it through soft silk.

I can feel her fingers now, muffled with silk, in my hair.

I was nervous when I got up and walked back to Eagle Court, the student housing where we live. Eric was out. I leant out of the window and saw him coming. He came into the room and at first seemed not to see me. We have a portable room, bits of this and that, futon, foldable table, framed portrait of his parents, one of Papa and Mama and me, taken when I was three, I sit in the middle, between them, my head against the wall, leaning back. That was all.

"OK?" he asked.

I didn't want to answer right off.

"You got to the falls?"

His eyes lit up.

"Tangled stuff hanging off trees, vines, bits of broken wood from summer houses. Yasu lifted as much as he could with his bare hands. I helped him scrape away the debris. And there under a rock lip."

He stopped short.

"Go on." I was goading him.

"It was beautiful Dora. You should have seen the hidden water!"

He came over and put his arms around me and I trembled. I felt so cold suddenly, as if the chill wind by the lake had entered me.

His voice was low. "So did you do what you had to?"

"Do what I had to?"

Like an idiot I repeated his words.

"You know, read the journal."

He was waiting, waiting for me to say something, fill him in, help us go on with our lives. But something in me refused. I couldn't help him, couldn't help us. But somehow my voice said:

"Mama went with him, sat with him at the water's edge."

"The Hudson?"

I nodded. But as Eric spoke an odd jealousy filled me. When had he and I last gone to the water's edge together, sat together, side by side, feeling the wind all around us? He went with Yasunari these days, walking, chatting. Perhaps that was safer than being with me.

"Dora, you OK?"

Eric had moved to the other side of the room, was standing against the counter, stirring his coffee cup.

"Uhu."

"Want to go out tonight? You haven't seen Yasu's pictures yet."

"Sure."

"So we'll eat something at the cafe?"

I turned away from him. I was happy when I saw him move towards his computer. It was his way of forgetting me. He had maps, graphs, baroque doodles marking wind and water, light that plotted its own death through speed, experiments with sense that revealed change, the vanishing of matter, natural entropy. I didn't want to talk to him any more, at least not just yet. Mama and that man she thought she loved—what is the difference between "thought she loved" and "loved'?—were too much inside me.

And my head felt warm, feverish even.

Did they walk when the plum blossoms came out in Riverside Park?

Twilight already and Mama and he held hands, saw twisted trunks of the plum trees, bark turned indigo in the half light, the showy pink petals.

But how could they have walked alone at twilight? I was so young and could not be left alone. Dinner had to be cooked before Papa returned. Perhaps someone stayed with me, Grandma, or Dominique who sometimes babysat. Or was it broad daylight when they strolled, rubbing shoulders with young mothers, derelicts, teen dropouts. Hands linked in sunlight, making their way carefully to the river.

But how could they have gotten close to water?

There is no openness there, to the Hudson. It is fenced off, with metal and wire. Waves grow rough as wind beats off the condominiums of New Jersey, off the scarred edges of the Palisades.

What did his hand feel like as she held it? Did she clasp it tight, or let it fall free? He had a mole on his right thumb. I know, somehow. Was it something she said to me?

So he was her secret life. Mama's other life all those years I was growing up. Just once, when I was ten, I saw them together sitting side by side on a wooden bench. The leavcs around them were dark green, clenched. A cold wind blew. She was pressed up close to him. His hair was all grey. I think he was shorter than her. I did not see his face.

I told Eric about it.

"They were sitting side by side on a bench. I was out playing ball with Wanda. I don't think they saw me. She didn't in any case."

He waited, saying nothing. I didn't know what to add. What would have happened if I had gone up and spoken to Mama? What could she have said. "Come Dora, come and say hello." Would she have murmured that? Or turned her face as I approached, pretending not to see?

I started scribbling on a bit of paper, balled it up and threw it into the trash heap. Eric fished it out. Smoothed it with his palms. His palms were slow, heavy.

"Dora, why?"

"Why what?"

"Why throw it away? It's your mother isn't it?"

He held it away at arm's length so the light washed over it. "And is that you?"

I had finished the outline of her, but not the small shape. It was an unfinished child, half the mother's size, the back not drawn so the blankness pressed in from behind. Blank white paper.

I did not have the courage to say, yes, Eric, yes.

I turned away from him, feeling my eyes wet.

With Mama and Papa split, what family did I have? I put out my hand and touched Eric on the cheek.

"Eric," I murmured. "I can't make pictures, you know that, don't you?" But the words only grazed the truth.

What I really wanted to tell him was how the waters of the Hudson, that dark river she faced, beat into me.

The cafe was warm, cups of tea steaming, a bowl of fried wafers, the window panes misted over. Covering the table was white paper, the kind kids draw on. And a stack of crayons, half chewed. There were some graduate students in the back of the cafe, and a child too, I heard its voice. I say "its" deliberately. At three or four who can tell? Mama used to walk me to school in the mornings when I was that age. I'd put my hand in hers, feel her bare palm. Then she'd laugh, make me pull my gloves on, the purple felt ones I loved.

"Dora, why don't you draw any more?"

Eric was staring at me, as if we had never met before. What was it with him?

"Dora, we could get pencils, paper. Look," he shoved the pack of crayons towards me. He seemed so eager. Yasunari was staring at me too.

"Wake, wake," he murmured.

I could feel my heart beating. Thump, thump, like a fish flapping its tail against a flat stone in the lake.

"We could get charcoal, Dora, you might like that. Look!" And Eric held up a stick he had got out of Yasunari's backpack.

I shook my head.

"Why? Why not draw? I do."

Yasunari said this quite delicately. He pointed behind his head. All around the walls were Yasunari's charcoal drawings, the latest exhibit of them in the only gallery he could find.

One of the images drew me. I could lose myself in it. There was a great deal to be lost in.

"Yasunari, its you isn't it in that picture?"

For some reason Eric was tapping his foot hard, as if he didn't want me to ask.

"That's me with Grandma rooting for coal."

"Coal?"

"Sure, to keep warm. Internment camp, Dora. Before you were born. Before your mother came to this country. Southern Idaho. The men threw a whole pile of coal in the middle of the yard and everyone had to jump for it. We got very little. It was bitterly cold in the nights. Grandma felt it. She made us children huddle by her, to warm her skin. In the morning, before the others woke up, she took me out, made me walk by her.

"'You have good eyes Yasunari,' she'd say, 'good eyes my child.'"

"I scraped the ground with my eyes for bits of coal others had missed. I can still see those black glittering bits. Like your eyes, Dora. They're from your mother, right? Where is she now, your mother? She's Indian, no? Indian?"

"Yes, she's Indian."

He pressed me: "Where is she now, in India?"

"New York."

"And your dad?"

"He's there too, but living apart. He talks of moving to Connecticut."

"Ah, the green fields, green dollars of Connecticut."

Yasunari's voice rose as if he were going to break into song.

"Yasu, here's some tea."

Eric was pouring out half of his own green tea into Yasunari's mug. Empty mug man Yasunari called himself in jest. He was on unemployment, on disability too for damages sustained in the soul, as he put it, from internment camp.

"Look at that picture!"

He was speaking to me.

"Notice the sun and stars?"

"Yes," I murmured, ever so softly. I put my hand next to Eric's, hoping they would touch, accidentally. Then I inched my hand closer so I could feel the warmth of him.

"Now why do you think I put the sun and the stars together? I'll tell you why. So that the golden eagle could soar. We know things Dora, Columbus never knew. I saw it first in the camp in southern Idaho. Desert, dry, blue air, sun and stars smooshed together and then the plane, zooming down. With bombs in its belly. Tracking us out. I was seven in 41. I wanted to hide out in the bathroom. No, my sister said we couldn't use the bathrooms till ten-thirty in the morning."

"Why?"

"Because Sis said they had to take out the hanging bodies. Suicide? Yes, yes, my people keep these things quiet. Camp, my dear child, was no Hayakawa picnic."

I felt Eric lift his palm and set it over mine. There was a heat there I needed. My hand was breathing under his, so still, all the pores breathing.

"O Yasu," I said, watching his mouth move, his lips tremble, not hearing him any more. There was grey in his beard. He was about the age Mama's lover would be.

"What adjustments we make, right? Now you my young Eric will perhaps one day understand. You too, Dora. What other family do we have?"

How slow and sad his voice was now, as he hunched over his tea cup. I held onto Eric's hand, listening as Yasunari went on:

"Our foremothers and forefathers came from Asia. The golden eagle came of Krishna's hands, it rises above the lost tribes of Asian America."

"Yasu, I think I want to see your waterfall picture."

I shifted my hand away from Eric's grasp. Pulled the thin black cardigan about me. It was the one Eric had given me for my birthday. I chose black so I could work in it, and the scrapings of charcoal, or the dark inks I favoured, wouldn't show.

I wanted to rest my eyes on a simpler image Yasu had made. It had hung above our bed for awhile, on loan. An untitled piece, a child, head bobbing in the waterfall, a single hand raised. Black ink, brushed against white paper. There was a gap where the child's ribcage might have been.

I moved towards the knot of people in the back of the cafe, not wanting to hear Yasu's voice. I didn't want to be the burial ground for his rage. I would leave it to Eric to calm him down, talk of wind tunnels and blasts of light, or what was new with Apu, Homer Simpson's pal or how far Kramer's purple hair in the last Seinfeld show stuck out.

I took my purse with me as I strolled around the cafe. I could feel the hard shape of Mama's notebook through the canvas.

Back home that night, I took her notebook out and set it on top of the fridge. Only later did it come back to me that I had put it where the ink bottle had been in Mama's kitchen, right on the fridge corner, above the stove and those bare flames.

The next morning, it was Eric's idea, and perhaps it was all my talk of the water that did it, we went all three to Lake Mendota. Yasu called it "a healing trip." I wondered what Eric might have told him of my morning. Or perhaps it was just Yasu's memory strained through layers of black ink and charcoal, stirring.

There were blades of grass by the lake. I bent myself low, the two men watching me. I became a curved thing, a bonsai tree with a load of brilliant black blossoms. I straightened up slowly feeling as if Mama were already dead.

I wanted to say something clear about Papa and Mama, about family. I wanted to say something about stealing her notebook. About making my own history. But there was no time.

For by the shores of that midwestern lake Yasunari of the coal-blackened eyes started singing ever so softly—a song he had made up about children in the desert. Then he took a piece of metal where it lay by his shoe and he made a music that Eric and I holding hands, moving closer to the waters, tried to dance to.

Contributors

MEENA ALEXANDER was born in India and raised there and in North Africa. She has published both poetry and prose widely and her works have been translated into many languages including Malayalam, Arabic, Italian, German and Spanish. She has published several volumes of poetry, including *River and Bridge* (TSAR, 1996). Her most recent work is the novel *Manhattan Music* (Mercury House, 1997). She lives in New York City.

ANITA RAU BADAMI is the author of *Tamarind Mem* (Penguin, 1996). She lives in Vancouver.

SHAUNA SINGH BALDWIN was born in Montreal, Canada and grew up in India. She is the author of *English Lessons and Other Stories* (Goose Lane Editions, 1996). Her stories have been published in magazines in India, the United States and Canada, and broadcast on CBC Radio. Among the awards she has received are the 1997 CBC Radio/Canada Council Literary Award, the 1995 Writers' Union of Canada Award, and the national Shastri Award (Silver Medal) for English Prose (India). Her novel *What the Body Remembers* will be published by Nan Talese/Doubleday and Knopf Canada in Fall 1999. She lives in Milwaukee, Wisconsin.

CHAYA BHUVANESWAR grew up in an immigrant community in New York City. She graduated from Yale University in 1993, where she received a Henfield Transatlantic Review Writing Award for short stories. At Oxford, on a Rhodes Scholarship, she studied Sanskrit. Her writing has appeared in various magazines. She is currently writing a novel, coediting a book about social activism by and for South Asians abroad, and hoping to provide medical care to uninsured and homeless people after her medical training at Stanford.

SHREE GHATAGE was born in Bombay, India and came to Canada from

Wales in 1983. She began writing creatively in 1992 in St John's, Newfoundland. Her poetry and short fiction have appeared in numerous literary journals across Canada. Her linked collection of short stories, *Awake When All the World Is Asleep* (House of Anansi, 1997), was shortlisted for several awards and won the 1998 Thomas H Radall Atlantic Fiction Prize. She now lives in Calgary where she is working on a novel.

LAKSHMI GILL was born in the Philippines of Indian/Spanish-Filipina parents and arrived in Vancouver in 1964 for her MA after her studies in the United States. Among her books are *During Rain, I Plant Chrysanthemums* (1966), *Mind Walls* (1970), and *Novena to St Jude Thaddeus* (1979). Her most recent book is *Returning the Empties* (TSAR, 1998), a selection of poems written in Canada since the 1960s. She has also written short stories and a novel, *The Third Infinitive* (TSAR, 1993). As well she has appeared in numerous magazines and anthologies.

GINU KAMANI, Bombay-born essayist and fiction writer, authored *Junglee Girl* (Aunt Lute Books, 1995), a collection of stories exploring sexuality, sensuality and power. She has published fiction and essays in various anthologies, literary journals, newspapers and magazines. Her essays and talks deal with gender and sexual self-knowledge in the context of the dual identities of hyphenated American subcultures. She is Visiting Writer in Fiction at Mills College, Oakland, California.

FARIDA KARODIA was born and raised in South Africa. Later she moved to Canada and now spends her time between the two countries. She is author of *Daughters of the Twilight* (The Women's Press, 1986), a runner-up for the Fawcett Prize, *Coming Home and Other Stories* (Heinemann, 1986), *A Shattering of Silence* (Heinemann, 1993) and *Against an African Sky and Other Stories* (TSAR, 1997). She is currently working on a novel.

AUSMA ZEHANAT KHAN was born in Leicester, England and immigrated to Canada in 1974. She graduated from the University of Toronto in 1991 and the University of Ottawa Faculty of Law in 1996, specializing in International Human Rights Law. She practices immigration law and has recently returned from a sojourn in the West Bank where she completed a collection of short stories. She writes poetry, short stories, plays and songs. She lives in the Toronto area.

MAYA KHANKHOJE, Mexican of Indian and Belgian origin, enjoys her work as a simultaneous interpreter in a UN agency in Montreal, but her real passion is writing. She has received a few awards for her poetry, fiction and essays. She is interested in peace, and in women's and environmental movements. Her daughters Nalini and Shanti are her greatest pride and joy.

GEETA KOTHARI is the editor of *Did My Mama Like to Dance? and Other Stories about Mothers and Daughters* (Avon). Her fiction and non-fiction have appeared in various journals and anthologies, including the *Kenyon Review,* the *New England Review*, *The Toronto South Asian Review* and *Her Mother's Ashes* (TSAR). She lives in Pittsburgh.

YASMIN LADHA has published three books: *Women Dancing on Rooftops: bring your belly close* (TSAR, 1997), a collection of prose-poems, essays and documentary fictions ; a chapbook, *Bridal Hands on the Maple* (DisOrientation, Second Wedneday Press, 1992); and a collection of short stories set in Tanzania, India and Canada, *Lion's Granddaughter and Other Stories* (NeWest, 1992). Currently she teaches and writes out of Chonju, South Korea. She is working on a collection of poetic fictions.

SUNAINA MAIRA teaches Asian American studies among other things. She is coeditor of *Contours of the Heart: South Asians Map North America* (Asian American Writers' Workshop/Temple University Press, 1996), an anthology that received the American Book Award in 1997. Her fiction has appeared in various journals in the United States. In New York City she has helped to organize Youth Solidarity Summer, a progressive summer programme for South Asian youth in the United States and Canada. She has also learnt to do club bhangra.

SHANI MOOTOO was born in Ireland and grew up in Trinidad. She is the author of *Out on Main Street* (Press Gang Publishers, 1993) a collection of short stories, and *Cereus Blooms at Night* (Press Gang, 1996), a novel, which was shortlisted for the 1997 Giller Prize. Her poetry and other writings have been anthologized in several publications, and she has written and directed several videos. Her visual art—paintings and photo-based works—is exhibited internationally. She divides her time between Vancouver, British Columbia, and Brooklyn, New York.

UMA PARAMESWARAN was born in India and came to Canada in 1966. She has written numerous critical articles on postcolonial literature and is the author of several volumes of creative writing, most recently, *Sons Must Die and Other Plays* published in India (1998). "The Icicle" is one of a collection of linked stories in progress entitled *Maru and the Maple Leaf.*

She teaches English at the University of Winnipeg.

ROSHNI RUSTOMJI was born in Bombay, India and has lived, studied and worked in India, Pakistan, Lebanon, the United States and Mexico. Her short stories and essays have appeared in various journals and anthologies in the United States and Canada. She has coedited *Blood into Ink: South Asian and Middle Eastern Women Write War* (Westview, 1994) and edited *Living in America: Fiction and Poetry by South Asian American Writers* (Westview, 1995) and *Encounters: People of Asian Descent in the Americas* (Rowman and Littlefield, 1999). She is professor emerita, Sonoma State University, and a visiting scholar at the Center for Latin American Studies, Bolivar House, Stanford University.

TANYA SELVARATNAM is an artist and activist based in New York. Her poetry and essays have appeared in numerous publications. She is performer with The Wooster Group and an organizer with the Ms Foundation for Women. She collaborated with Conway & Pratt Projects on "A Woman's Work Is Never Done," has worked with Anna Deavere Smith, and has taken her solo shows around the United States and abroad. The story in this anthology is dedicated to the memory of her father.

The Editor:

NURJEHAN AZIZ was born in Dar es Salaam, Tanzania, and immigrated to Canada in 1980. She is a cofounder of *The Toronto South Asian Review,* now *The Toronto Review,* of which she is an editorial board member, and she is also the publisher at TSAR Publications. She lives in Toronto.